I0618152

THE POISON PEN . . .

To millions of loyal readers, Myron Kane was a
great man, a genius, a truth-teller.

But to everyone who knew him personally,
Myron Kane was a man with the touch of death,
whose razor-edged pen could destroy a reputation, a life, a soul—and never hesitated to do so.

It was no surprise, then, that somebody decided
to prove once and for all that a knife, if buried
in human flesh, could be far deadlier than a
pen . . .

"Leslie Ford's reputation as one of the best mystery writers will be made even more secure"
—LOUISVILLE COURIER JOURNAL

ABOUT THE AUTHOR

LESLIE FORD has become one of the most widely read mystery writers in America. Her first novel was published in 1928 and since then she has written over forty others.

Miss Ford lives in Annapolis, Maryland.

Among her books are *False to Any Man, Old Lover's Ghost, The Town Cried Murder, The Woman in Black, Trial by Ambush, Ill Met by Moonlight, The Simple Way of Poison, The Clue of the Judas Tree, Three Bright Pebbles, Washington Whispers Murder* and *The Bahamas Murder Case.*

The Philadelphia Murder Story ∽

by LESLIE FORD

WILDSIDE PRESS

The Philadelphia Murder Story

Copyright © 1945, renewed 1972, by Zenith Brown.
All rights reserved.

Published by Wildside Press LLC
www.wildsidepress.com

1

The editors of *The Saturday Evening Post* have finally over-come what I think I may call their natural reluctance about telling the full story of the body they found in the goldfish pool in the entrance lobby of The Curtis Publishing Comany Building on Independence Square, in Philadelphia, last winter. The ribald cries that went up in the New York columns about sweeping out the editorial offices and finding more bodies, including illustrators and fiction writers, had nothing to do, they insist, with that decision.

If there was pressure on the editors to tell the story, in fact, it was probably brought by the *Ladies' Home Journal* and the *Country Gentleman*, who'd got tired of trying to explain that it had nothing to do with them—though neither, I'm told, has ever admitted the authorship of that interoffice memorandum entitled "Bring Out Your Dead" that was put up on the *Post* doors on the sixth floor.

This may all seem a little heartless now, but, as they said at the time, no one can go around asking for murder and expect tears to be shed when he gets it. I was, and in telling the story of what happened I still am, a little afraid that the people who write to the editors saying it must be Grace Latham who murders the victims herself, will now accuse them of wanting to get rid of this victim and calling me in to do it for them. It does seem obvious that a widow on what someone once kindly called the glamorous side of forty, living in Georgetown, District of Columbia, should not, in the ordinary nature of things, be constantly stumbling over corpses. On the other hand, it seems only fair to say I never did, until Col. John Primrose and Sgt. Phineas T. Buck became a Hydra-headed figure in my life. If people are suspicious of me, I can truthfully say there are times when I've been a little suspicious of Colonel Primrose and his sergeant.

5

I've sometimes thought that when they retired from the Army (92nd Engineers) and started doing private inquiry for various governmental agencies, they set out to find what I hope it's all right to call a fall guy, and found me living right across from them on P Street. It seems I was pretty much of a natural, or at least I certainly was in the business of the body in the pool and *The Saturday Evening Post*. And as for people constantly demanding why I don't marry Colonel Primrose and get it over with, the answer is simply that he's never actually asked me to, and I don't feel I know him well enough to suggest it myself.

In any case, I was responsible neither for the body's being put into the goldfish pool in The Curtis Building lobby nor for Colonel Primrose's being there to help get it out. The editors of *The Saturday Evening Post* are responsible for the whole thing. If they hadn't let Myron Kane do the profile of Judge Nathaniel Whitney, the marble-alabaster sanctuary of that lobby would never have been the scene of as astonishing a murder as ever turned a magazine inside out, and if they hadn't themselves got Colonel Primrose in when things first began to look odd, I doubt if anybody would have discovered who did it or why. Where Colonel Primrose is, Sergeant Buck follows as the night the day, and it was Buck who stated the whole responsibility in a very few words. Few for most people, I mean. For Sergeant Buck it was a full week's supply of his stringently rationed vocabulary, and the longest coherent statement I ever heard him make.

"If you lay down with dogs, you got to expect to get fleas," he said.

He may have had something more in mind than the editors of the *Post* consorting with Myron Kane, because he'd already said Colonel Primrose's being there in Philadelphia was a wild-moose chase, and he's almost as suspicious of anybody connected with the printed word as he is of women who are designing to marry his colonel. And he never actually got over his mistrust of the people on the *Post*. Being a black-jack-and-poker man himself, he could easily suspect anything of Bob Fuoss, the managing editor, and Art Baum, one of the associate editors, when he found out they wasted their lunch hour playing three-cushion billiards, and the fact that Fuoss had played with Willie Hoppe was only the slightest mitigation. Ben Hibbs, the editor, he got to like, I suppose because of the earthy grass roots Ben had trailed from Kansas, though certainly that wouldn't explain his attitude

6

toward Marion Turner, one of the two women editors on the *Post*. It was his deep conviction that she, at least, had nothing to do with the murder—or it was until he saw her lunching at the Downtown Club with Colonel Primrose. Black hair, gray-green eyes and magnolia-petal skin are excellent things in a woman, but not when one's colonel is so absorbed in conversation with them he forgets he's supposed to be at the city jail.

However, when Sergeant Buck first saw them, all pretty shattered, I may say, by sudden violent death in their own front door, the marble bust of Benjamin Franklin looking quietly down from his fluted pedestal while detectives, white-faced editors and a pair of startled paper and ink salesmen milled about, he and the pallid goldfish huddled at the far end of the oblong pool regarded them with much the same look in their clammy eyes. It was no doubt the most excitement they'd had in all their submerged and sunless lives. The goldfish, I mean. I don't know about the editors of the *Post*. And yet it was the editors who'd decided to have Myron Kane do the profile of Judge Nathaniel Whitney. The marble lobby, the pool with the water playing from shallow fountain urns, the goldfish, the great mosaic Dream Garden by Tiffany out of Maxfield Parrish will never seem so enchanted again. I've forgotten who it was said a lot of people had sweated blood crossing that lobby, going to interview an editor, but nobody had ever shed it there before.

2

Myron Kane had come back on the national scene after his notorious run-in with the military about evading censorship in the Near East. I'd read about him in a column syndicated from New York:

> Another foreign commentator has decided fairer fields are closer home. Myron Kane, pal of princes, potentates and premiers—but not generals—is around town. He's doing a piece for a national-circulation weekly on a Quaker City celeb. May be dull, may be a libel suit, depending on what table in snob Rittenhouse Square he picks his crumbs up at.

That was in November, and when I got back home to Georgetown for the Christmas holidays, I found a letter from Myron on my desk. It said:

> *Dear Grace:* I understand you have relatives by marriage in Philadelphia. If they include, or you otherwise know, that eccentric museum piece, Abigail Whitney, will you drop me a note of introduction? I understand she's taken her own name back, not being up to the mental effort of keeping her marital ventures in proper sequence. I'm doing a profile of her brother, Judge Nathaniel Whitney, for the Sat Eve Post, and I understand they've lived next door to each other and haven't spoken for years, so I can't meet her through him. If you ever get up there, give me a buzz and I'll buy you a stengah.
>
> MYRON KANE.

I did have relatives by marriage in Philadelphia, and some of them might be called museum pieces. Abigail Whitney was not one of them. I knew her very slightly, and that just from times I'd met her before I married Bill Latham, who came from there. After the plane crash that left me with two small sons, I seldom went back. In those days Abigail Whitney was in her late heyday and still very beautiful. My husband's family thought she was shocking, and no doubt she was, but being a Whitney kept doors open to her that her money couldn't have and that her four marriages and numerous escapades on both sides of the Atlantic should have locked and double-locked. She seemed to my generation to be a high wind, fresh if somewhat salty.

I didn't know her well, however, and I'd never seen her since, though I'd heard a lot of gossip about her, and tales of the jungle warfare she carried on with her brother from their foxholes next door to each other in Rittenhouse Square.

She wouldn't, furthermore, have known me from Adam, and if she'd been my best friend I wouldn't have sent Myron Kane an introduction to her. He seemed to have forgotten the time I came in once and found him reading a letter I'd left on my desk. It was from the wife of a cabinet member, and the fact that he was doing a piece on her husband seemed sufficient reason to him, if not to me, or to her when it came out in print.

But Myron hadn't got to be the pal of princes, potentates and premiers by letting what Sergeant Buck calls the amendities stand in his way. The special-delivery letter I got from Abigail Whitney one morning early in January was added evidence of that.

"Dear Child," it began, and it was scrawled at what looked like white heat in green ink across and around and crisscross on the blue paper. "I must have mislaid your Letter introducing your Friend Myron Kane, but of course I am Happy to have him here for your Sake, and I'm sure the Hotels are very crowded. I remember the Lathams very well, although I haven't seen any of them for Years, and always thought they were Estimable but Dull."

I could hardly have been more appalled. I knew Myron Kane had the effrontery of a brass elephant, but this was a fabrication out of such whole cloth that I doubt if even such an elephant would ever have thought of it.

"You know, of course," her letter went on, "he is doing a Profile of my Brother for *The Saturday Evening Post*, which I wish to say I no longer subscribe to since they have Changed the Cover, as in my Opinion it is like painting a

9

Bathing Beauty on Independence Hall, nor can I imagine a Sane Editor wanting a Profile or even a Rear View of my Brother, who, as you know, is a Scoundrel. But the Reason I am Writing is that your Friend is making a Great Deal of Trouble. The Children are Very Bitter about him."

As I'd never known anyone Myron did a story about who wasn't very bitter about him, I wasn't surprised at that. I read on, wondering if I'd find out who the children were:

"Monckton, who, you remember, was Very Wild, is coming back on leave today. Elsie, who married that Stuffed Shirt, Sam Phelps, whose Father made so much Money, must have sent for him, and I am very much Alarmed. Travis Elliot—you will recall our dear old friend, his father, Douglas Elliot, and his shocking Death, it was so Useless, my dear!— Travis is being very Sensible."

I did, as a matter of fact, recall Douglas Elliot. He was the Latham family lawyer, and his death was indeed shocking, because it was by his own hand. It was not only shocking, it was incomprehensible. He was one of the most prominent and respected men in Philadelphia. How useless it was, I didn't know, as there had never been anything but vague rumors about why he did it before it was all hushed up quickly and quietly. I had, however, heard there was a son who had carried on with a good deal of courage, and Travis Elliot, I gathered, must be that son.

"Travis does not think Laurel Frazier will be indiscreet about my Brother's affairs," Mrs. Whitney's letter continued. "Or did you know that Laurel Frazier has been my Brother's private Secretary for the past five years? And I can't myself believe Laurel's head has been turned by Myron Kane's attentions, which are very Marked, even if he is World Famous. She has too many reasons for being terribly Grateful to Travis. I expect they will be married very soon now. Even my Brother, I understand, has given up the Hope that his son Monk will Reform, and it was nothing but Wishful Thinking on his part that Monk and Laurel would be attracted to Each Other, as they always have quarreled."

Living in the babel of alphabetical pyramids on the Potomac as I do ought to make anyone at home in any rat race, no matter how complicated, but it hadn't me. I was as confused by this welter of names and cross purposes as if I'd never set foot in either Washington or Philadelphia. The one thing that was really clear to me was that if Myron Kane was paying marked attention to Laurel Frazier, who was the

10

private secretary of the man he was doing a profile about, it wasn't for herself alone. The attentions would be finished the day the profile was, and Travis Elliot could have back the girl who had so many reasons for being grateful to him. And the rest of them could go on being bitter.

I glanced over the last page of the letter.

"But the Point, dear Child, is that I wish you to come up here at once. Myron Kane has told me about a Policeman he says you are going to marry. Perhaps you or your Policeman can have some Influence on your Friend, Mr. Kane, as it is a very Serious Matter and you are Responsible for his being in my House. I shall expect you tomorrow. I cannot meet you, as I do not Now Leave the House."

It was signed, "Affectionately, Abigail Whitney," with a postscript that said, "My house is the Pink one in the Square, which I painted that Color to Annoy my Brother, and am unable to get workmen to do over until After the War. I will expect you to stay here with me.—A. W."

It was all very unfortunate, of course, I realized, but it certainly didn't seem to me that I could be held responsible for Myron Kane. If Abigail Whitney took strange men into her house because they said someone she could remember only vaguely, if at all, had written her a letter about them, it was her problem, not mine. She was old enough and worldly enough to know better. And as for my so-called policeman, he was already in Philadelphia, doing some kind of job for the United States Treasury, in reference, no doubt, to that grim date, March fifteenth. I wrote Mrs. Whitney, telling her I was sorry, I'd never sent Myron Kane to her, and if he'd ever been a friend of mine, he wasn't any longer. And that, I thought, was that.

But it wasn't. She was on the long-distance telephone before I got the letter in the mailbox next morning. Discursive and disjointed as the monologue that came over the wire was, several things were clear at the end of it. One was that Judge Whitney's son Monk had got home and was in no mood for nonsense. Another was that Myron Kane was on the point of ruining the whole family. By some curious mental process, Abigail Whitney had skipped from my being responsible for Myron Kane to my being responsible for Myron, *The Saturday Evening Post*, her brother's profile, and a great deal of sorrow, tribulation and heartbreak for everybody. But the appeal behind all of it was desperation. It was the desperation of an old woman suddenly caught in a

11

tangled web she'd helped to weave and now was powerless to get out of. It was extraordinary how starkly implicit her despair and fear of something was in her repeated denials of it. It seemed so strange, too, because I would have thought Judge Whitney was one man whose life had no dark places for fear of exposure to cause such desperate anxiety.

3

Police detectives I've heard talk are always saying, "It was a funny coincidence that broke that case," or "It was just that I got all the breaks that time." It seems to me to happen too often not to imply something else. It's almost as if a powerful magnetic field forms itself out of the concentrated stuff of guilt, drawing the people involved in the pattern unconsciously together, without apparent reason or awareness, and that when the pattern is once definitely established, the seeming coincidences that finally make a coherent whole really are not accidental at all.

Or there's no other way I can explain what happened the day I went up to Philadelphia. It took me so long to get Colonel Primrose on the phone up there, and tell him I was coming and about Myron, that I missed the train I was planning to take. I took the three o'clock.

It was twenty minutes late into the 30th Street Station, and my shuttling across to the Broad Street Station was just as much a part of the magnetic field. It's the first time I'd ever done it, and why I suddenly thought I'd have a better chance for a taxi there, I haven't an idea. And if all those things hadn't happened I wouldn't have seen Myron Kane or met Albert Toplady.

I saw Myron by the newsstand. He's tall and slightly stoop-shouldered, with curly black hair and always immaculately well tailored, usually with a Homburg and fitted overcoat and stick, and generally looking as if he were just setting out to meet a prince or a potentate. I started over, and then I saw there was a girl there, talking to him. That in itself was unusual. Myron's taste in women, as I knew it in Washington, had always run to the wide-eyed and not very bright who listened while he did the talking. This girl's hair was a soft auburn nimbus brushed back from her broad forehead, touching the collar of her Persian-lamb Chesterfield coat. Her eyes seemed to be a sort of odd gray-blue, though just then the pupils were so dilated that the irises were hardly visible. She had high cheekbones and a pointed chin, and her face was pale with the intensity of some emotion that certainly had nothing to do with Myron's personal charm.

I heard her voice before I saw more than her burnished hair. ". . . can't do it, Myron, you can't!" she was saying. "I'll do everything to stop you. It's all my fault and it means everything to me. Everything, I tell you!"

Her face and voice were alive with passionate determination. I started to move behind Myron to go out the other door, and then I was caught in the crowd of people streaming in, beginning the homeward rush of a city of commuters emptying itself at the close of the business day.

Myron Kane's Oxford-out-of-Virginia accent and slightly superior tone seemed shockingly casual compared with the girl's intensity.

"All right," he said. "Marry me and I'll skip it."

"Marry you!" It was a sharp, incredulous gasp. "You're crazy. I'm going to marry Travis Elliot. You know it."

"Oh, no," he said easily. "People don't marry for gratitude any longer. You haven't got any reason anyway to be——"

"It's not gratitude! It's——"

I was jostled toward the door just then, and went on to the taxi entrance, catching just a glimpse of the two bright red spots that had flared up in her cheeks, and her eyes shining with anger. If she was going to marry Travis Elliot, she was obviously Judge Whitney's secretary, Laurel Frazier. I tried to get another look, but the door closed behind me.

It was cold outside, and across Penn Square the sleet was coming down in slanting black lines through the maze of moving headlights. It was just then I was first aware of the gray-haired, wizened little man, his overcoat turned up around his neck, standing there also waiting for a cab. I had an instant fleeting impression that he'd been back there inside and had seen me eavesdropping, but I dismissed that as just my guilty conscience.

I said, "Rittenhouse Square," when the taxi starter asked me where I was going, and he turned back. "Wasn't you going to Rittenhouse Square, buddy?"

It was the little man in the gray coat. He nodded, sidled forward and waited for me to get in the cab.

14

"Rittenhouse Square!" the starter called again.

The door swung open and Myron Kane came out alone. He raised his hand toward the starter, stiffened abruptly, turned and strode rapidly back into the station. If I could have seen his face after he'd started toward the cab, I'd have thought he'd recognized me and was making an escape, but he couldn't have seen my face any more than I could his, and he'd hardly recognize me from the knees down. He must have thought of something he hadn't said to Laurel Frazier, I decided.

The driver put his flag down. "Where to?" he asked.

I gave Abigail Whitney's number on 19th Street. The driver looked at the little man. Something seemed to have happened to him. His jaw was working, but no sound came from his lips.

"Just . . . the corner of Walnut Street," he said at last.

He sat bolt upright as we nosed into the traffic, and then he glanced at me, not furtively at all, but with a kind of anxious curiosity and an obvious desire to say something if he could get up courage enough. At last he did.

"Are you . . . going to Mrs. Whitney's?" he stammered.

"Yes," I said.

"Do you know Mr. Kane, by any chance? The—the great foreign correspondent?"

I looked at him blankly. It would have been an extraordinary thing at any time, but after the last few moments it was incredible.

"Why, yes, I do," I said.

"Then would you mind giving him this?" He fumbled in his pocket and brought out an envelope. "It's a—a letter for him," he said lamely.

"May I ask why you didn't give it to him yourself?" I inquired, bewildered, but curious too.

"Was that him talking to Miss Frazier?" The envelope shook a little in his hand.

"Do you know Miss Frazier?" I asked it, thinking what an odd kind of cat-and-mouse game we seemed to be playing with each other.

"Oh, no," he said quickly. "I know who she is. Her father was a—a great doctor. Everybody, poor and rich, loved him. I used to see her with him sometimes. But I don't know her."

The little man spoke very hurriedly, as if trying to correct at once an idea I'd got that he was pretending to be better than he was.

15

It was rather pathetic, because she hadn't looked like the kind of person who'd think it was presumptuous of him to say he knew her.

"Mr. Kane is staying right in the house with Mrs. Whitney," he said, with a kind of simple awe that was almost startling.

I tried not to smile. "You do know him?"

He flushed uncomfortably. "Oh, no. I just . . . follow his writings. He's wonderful, don't you think so?"

As I couldn't say what I thought of Myron at the moment to someone who put him in the ranks of the major gods, I nodded.

"And you'll give him this?" He handed the letter to me.

"I'll be glad to," I said, taking it.

"He's doing an article about Judge Whitney," he said, after a moment. "I read that in the papers. I used to see Judge Whitney too. I could tell him lots of things about him."

"Good or bad?" I asked, as casually as I could. He looked at me so blankly that I let it go. "What if he isn't there? He was in the station. He might be going away."

He looked apprehensively at the letter in my hand. "Just put it in the fire," he said. "It isn't really important. I wouldn't want to bother anybody."

The driver slowed down at the corner of the square; the little man fumbled with the door handle.

"I could send it back to you," I said. He got out.

"My name's Toplady—Albert Toplady," he said hastily. "Just Quaker Trust Company—that'll get me. I'll be much obliged——"

The light had changed, the driver was waiting impatiently, and the cars behind us were, too, so I didn't hear the rest of it. I looked back through the window, but Albert Toplady was lost in the stream of people hurrying home from work through the sleety darkness.

The taxi skidded around the corner and to the curb in front of Abigail Whitney's house. I caught my breath and got out. The house wasn't pink. In the icy rain, it was the color of raspberry sherbet, and the soot had left black streaks hanging from the window ledges. I rang the doorbell and noticed I wasn't alone on the step. A squirrel sat there, old and wet, twitching his moth-eaten tail impatiently, looking up at the door. It didn't seem extraordinary to be standing there with him, and I wasn't surprised when the butler, as old and in a coat as moth-eaten, took a walnut out of his pocket

16

and gave it to him before he gave me a childlike, vacant smile and picked up my bag.

"Mrs. Latham? Madam is in her room." His voice had the remote quality of the very deaf.

I followed him inside. The house was very handsome and surprisingly modern—more surprisingly so, in fact, than I then realized. There were mirrored panels in the soft beige walls. We went up a marble staircase curving gracefully to a wide foyer on the second floor. On the side wall were two more large mirrored panels, and in the space between them a decorative recess with a carved shell ceiling. A paneled library stretched across the back. The door to the room at the front stood open, and the voices coming from it, and not sounding very amicable, stopped abruptly as we came up.

"Madam's room," the butler said.

If the squirrel didn't surprise me, Abigail Whitney did. It hadn't occurred to me, when she'd said she did not now leave the house, that it was anything but another of the vagaries she was famous for, but in the wide room overlooking the square she sat propped up in yellow satin cushions against the yellow satin-upholstered back of an Empire swan-sleigh bed. There was a green satin cover over the blanket, and otherwise nothing of the bedroom apparent around her. The room was a drawing room, elegantly furnished, but crowded, as if she'd brought as much as possible out of her glamorous past to be there with her.

The windows by the bed bowed slightly, so that she had a full view of the square, and I saw that she had more than that. Outside were two mirrors. One was an old Philadelphia custom I'd heard of but never seen. It was placed so that the ladies of a day when they were less mobile and more ladylike could see who was at the door in the street. The other was fixed at an angle that showed the brownstone front next door. Bed or no bed, Abigail Whitney could keep track not only of her own entrance but her brother's too.

"Oh, Dear Child," she said as she held out her hand to me.

I was aware there were other people in the room, but it was the pair of blank blue eyes in the saffron face of the old woman that focused my attention. They were blank and vague, but they sharpened with surprising intentness as she took me in from head to foot, and without a glimmer of remembrance or recognition.

"Dear Child," she repeated. "You haven't changed at All. I'm so Happy to see you Again."

17

I wouldn't have remembered her either. There was no trace of the extraordinary beauty she'd had once. She had on a black padded silk coat with an enormous burst of diamonds in the white ruching at her neck. Her nose was sharp as a hawk's and her hair was a preposterous dye job of brilliant henna in a short fuzz all over her head.

Abigail Whitney's feud with her brother didn't, it seemed, extend to his family.

"You remember my Brother's children, dear Child," she said. She emphasized words the way she capitalized them when she wrote. "Elsie, and Monk, and Elsie's husband, Sam. No, not Sam. No one remembers Sam, because no one knew him. Sam is Respectable. . . . Come, dear Boy, I want you to meet Mrs. Latham. . . . This is Sam Phelps, dear Child."

Respectable was the word, I thought as Sam same forward. He was very bald, with a waxed mustache, pince-nez in his hand, a high wing collar, a black coat and knife-edge-pressed, gray-striped trousers. He was forty, I imagined, and looked as if he had all the prejudices he would ever need.

We spoke to each other. There was nothing cordial about Sam, but there wasn't about any of the others. Philadelphians, a famous Philadelphian once said, are taller and fairer than the Chinese but not so progressive, and, he might have added, not so warmly effusive as the English. In this instance, however, looking around at the three others nodding stiffly to me, I wasn't surprised, for they'd obviously been in the course of a first-class family row.

"And Travis, dear Child. You remember Travis Elliot."

The son of Mrs. Whitney's old friend who had taken his own life seemed much more at home than Sam Phelps did, and furthermore, I thought, he did not look as if it would take any particular gratitude to make a girl delighted to marry him. He was tall and attractive and about thirty-five, and looked definitely what Mrs. Whitney had said he was, a successful young Philadelphia lawyer. I looked at Judge Whitney's son Monk with more interest. He was at least old enough to be a major in the Marine Corps, and from the double row of ribbons, two of them star-sprinkled, over the pocket of his tunic, he had seen action in places far remote from Rittenhouse Square. His face was broad, rugged, tough and weather-beaten, and so sun-bronzed that his gray eyes looked very light. He had shaggy eyebrows and a big, generous mouth, and what was left of his hair after a G.I. haircut was dark and crisp.

18

I wondered whether he'd really been wild or just head-strong. He looked disciplined enough now, and he couldn't have been more than twenty-seven or eight, and people don't get to be majors in the Marine Corps—out there—without something.

After he'd spoken to me, Sam Phelps went abruptly to the side of the bed. "We must be going, I'm afraid. Mustn't tire you."

"Good-by, dear Boy," Abigail Whitney said, hastily and with considerable relief, I thought. "Good-by, Elsie." She turned to me. "Do sit down, my dear. What is that you have in your hand?"

I wasn't aware at all that I was still holding Myron Kane's fan mail.

"It's just a letter for Myron Kane," I said. "A little man named Toplady gave it to me in the taxi."

I thought even then there was a short silence in the room.

Mrs. Whitney spoke quickly, "Wasn't that a book? *Toplady on a Totem Pole?* . . . Travis, where is Elsie's coat? She has a Meeting."

Elsie Phelps spoke sharply. "I'm not leaving this house, Aunt Abby—not until you've told us what's in that profile of father. You know what's in it. We want to know too."

I'd already got the impression that Elsie Whitney Phelps was the focal point of the seething disturbance in the room. It seemed to me a fine instance of natural selection that she was Sam's wife. She was thirty, probably, sandy-haired, with rather pale blue eyes, and not unattractive, in a green tweed suit and hat that she'd had a long time and would continue to have till she gave them to some extraordinary deserving and respectable indigent. There was a simple conviction of superiority about her that was not complacent at all, but just the natural consequence of having been born in Philadelphia, a Whitney, endowed at birth with the knowledge of right and wrong and no sense of humor.

Mrs. Whitney held out her hand to me. "Elsie's a Tiresome Woman, Dear Child," she said. "You have no interest in this——"

Elsie Phelps cast me an angry glance. "She's a friend of Myron Kane's, isn't she? I'll tell you what's happened, Aunt Abby. You've been sitting up here for years trying to make trouble for father, and now it's backfired."

Her husband and her brother both started to speak, and she turned on them hotly. "If you had any pride you'd do

19

something, Monk Whitney!" Her voice rose. "It doesn't make any difference to Sam. He doesn't realize that people in our position can't have mud thrown at them! And Travis— you'd think Travis would understand how I feel. If he wasn't trying to defend Laurel Frazier——"

"Keep Laurel out of this," Monk said curtly. "It wasn't her fault."

"Whose fault was it? If it hadn't been for her, Myron Kane wouldn't ever have thought of doing a story on father! He was mad about her in London last summer—father told me so. He says himself it's the only reason he ever came here!"

Travis Elliot said, "If I were you, I'd shut up, Elsie."

She turned furiously on him. "You're a fine one to talk! After the smear campaign people put you through, everybody'd think you'd——" She stopped short, in a sudden silence that struck the room like a clap of thunder. "I'm sorry, Travis," she said quickly. "I didn't mean that. I shouldn't have——"

"It's all right," he said. His face was flushed a little. "Just get it straight, though. Nobody ever smeared me. People were damned decent to me. And if Laurel made a mistake, she didn't do it on purpose. If you'd stow this holier-than-thou business, you'd make fewer yourself. I think you've said plenty, and if I were you I'd go home."

Mrs. Whitney was lying back on her yellow pillows.

"All right," Elsie Phelps said. When she looked at her aunt, her eyes were sharp pinpoints of anger. "When Aunt Abby feels better, maybe she'll tell you what was in the sealed document Laurel gave Myron Kane. And why she's so frantic to get it back."

Mrs. Whitney's hand moved slightly on the green blanket cover.

Monk Whitney turned abruptly. "What sealed document?"

He'd been looking out the window at the mirror reflecting his father's doorway. I saw in it, as he must have done, the slim, auburn-crowned figure of the girl there, visible in the light from the hall as she took the key out of the lock and slipped quickly inside.

"What document?" he repeated.

Elsie Phelps laughed shortly. "Nobody ever heard of anything. Nobody knows anything. If Myron Kane was in this conspiracy of silence, it would be lovely. But he isn't. You'd better go back and get another ribbon in the Pacific; you've never been any good anywhere else. You can kill Japs, but you haven't got what it takes to keep one news reporter from disgracing your own family."

He looked at her silently. There was an angry flush on Travis Elliot's face as he turned and threw his half-smoked cigarette abruptly into the fire.

"I think we'd better go," Sam Phelps said nervously. He went to Monk Whitney and put out his hand. "Sorry. Elsie's upset. All this war work she's doing——"

Monk Whitney smiled rather grimly. "I'm used to it, Sam. So long."

Sam Phelps made a stiff bow to me and followed his wife out. There was complete silence in the room for an instant. Abigail Whitney opened her eyes then.

"Elsie is Very Trying," she said. "I've always found it best not to listen to her. I Concentrate my Mind on Something Else." She raised her hand toward me. "Dear Child, you want to go to your room. It's upstairs, in back, or is it front? It's wherever Myron isn't, and I'm sure you can tell. Come down Again soon, won't you?" She went on without a stop, "Travis, dear Boy, you must have a great many Things to do. I won't keep you any longer—and close the door, it's very drafty in here."

Travis Elliot followed me out into the hall and did close the door. Then he looked at me with a smile. "You'll get used to her."

"I hadn't realized she was an invalid," I said.

He nodded. "She slipped on the ice eight years ago, and she's never walked since."

His face sobered. "It was coming from my father's funeral. I've always felt sort of—— Well, you know. That's not why I come here, though. I'm nuts about her. . . . Oh, I forgot."

He turned back and knocked on the door, and I went on upstairs, to find the back room, or was it the front.

I knew the instant I pushed open the door that it wasn't the back. My feet had made no sound on the thickly carpeted stairs. The girl kneeling on the floor beside the wastepaper basket, her back to me, her hair a shower of molten copper in the light from the desk lamp, was too intently occupied to be aware the door was opening until it was too late.

She started violently and flashed her head around, a breathless gasp parting her red lips, the defiance that had

21

darted into her eyes changing to alarmed dismay at the sight of someone she didn't know. I must have looked just as startled myself.

"Who . . . are you?" she stammered. Her face flushed crimson as she got to her feet in the middle of the litter of papers from Myron Kane's wastebasket. Some of them were still in crumpled balls, and the ones she'd smoothed out to read had partly finished paragraphs on them, obviously discarded by Myron Kane as unsatisfactory.

"I'm Grace Latham," I said. "I'm sorry. I was looking for my room."

She took a step toward me. "You're a friend of Myron's, aren't you? He's talked about you. I'm Laurel Frazier. Maybe you can do something. That's why Mrs. Whitney asked you to come, isn't it?"

She stood there, her back to the desk, slim and really lovely, and still startled, the color in her cheeks heightened, her chin raised, not defiant now, so much as defensive. She didn't look more than eighteen, in the Quakerish gray wool dress with a narrow white collar tied in a small bow at the throat. Her eyes were wide-set and the curious gray-blue of wood hyacinths, flecked with black. I could understand Travis Elliot and Myron Kane wanting to marry her more easily than I could Judge Whitney having had her as private secretary for five years. She looked more like a frightened, lovely child than an efficient young woman one took on a mission to London.

It was an extraordinarily embarrassing situation for both of us, and I didn't really know what to say.

"I'm not a friend of Myron's when he takes things that don't belong to him," I replied. I don't know why I added, "It's the—the document, I suppose?"

It seemed a silly thing to call it, but that was apparently what it was, the way they all referred to it.

The pulse in her throat quickened as she stared at me. "He . . . told you?"

I shook my head. "Judge Whitney's daughter. Mrs. Phelps."

"Elsie." It was hardly more than a whisper, and the color ebbed sharply from her cheeks. "Then she was listening. I knew she was. I told him so."

"Told——"

"Judge Whitney." She said it mechanically. "Oh, it's so awful! Now everybody—— And it's my fault!"

22

She turned her head away, trying to keep back the tears that were glistening along her thick black lashes. I looked around the room. She'd done a thorough if slapdash job of searching it. The drawers of the dresser and the desk were pushed back crooked and the books and papers on the desk were pretty helter-skelter.

"If only I'd been careful!" she said. "And he's being so wonderful about it. He keeps saying not to worry, it isn't my fault and it'll turn up somewhere in the library, but I know he's terribly upset. He's gone through everything over and again, at night after I've gone. But it isn't there. I've looked everywhere."

"What . . . is it?" I asked.

She shook her head. "I don't know. All I know is it's something that will . . . hurt somebody terribly." She tried to control her voice. "It's worse because it wasn't his. It's something she gave him to keep." She nodded down toward Abigail Whitney's room. "She gave it to him because she said she could trust him not to open it better than she could herself."

"Then she doesn't—neither of them knows what's in it?"

"She may now. Maybe Myron told her. She always finds everything out, someway."

I wondered if that could explain her sudden desperate fear when she'd talked to me over the phone that morning. She surely hadn't known, whatever it was, when she wrote to me.

"If only I hadn't been so smart," Laurel Frazier was saying helplessly. "It was me that suggested it. I wanted people to know about my boss, because I'm so proud of him. And he said I could give Myron a file of his old records, and it must have been in them."

She stopped short, her slim body stiffening as if an electric charge had gone through it, the color rising in her cheeks again. She was looking past me at the door, and I turned quickly. Monk Whitney was there, looking down at the littered floor. If he was surprised, there was nothing in his manner to show it. He came on into the room.

"It didn't occur to you to check through the file before you gave it to him?" he said calmly. "Where's the old Frazier efficiency they talk about, Coppertop?"

She flared up passionately. "Quit calling me Coppertop! And I don't need you to tell me what I should have done! I know it. I started to, but we were busy, and they were all

23

before my time. I know it's my fault. I'm not trying to pretend it isn't!"

"Myself, I don't see what all the row's about," he said imperturbably. "If the old man's got a dark streak in the past, I'm all for it. If it's too dark, the *Post* isn't going to publish it. They aren't running a scandal sheet. Nobody'll be hurt."

"You don't know Myron Kane!" Laurel retorted hotly. "He's so clever, they'll never know what he's doing. It'll sound perfectly all right. I know. He told me in London last year he'd got even with lots of people that way."

Monk Whitney shook his head. "Who's he got to get even with around here, Dear Child?"

"Everybody. Sam and Elsie treated him like a police reporter with the smallpox. And he's sensitive as a child; he's always trying to cover up to keep from being hurt. Travis was horrid, and you've been just as bad. Patronizing and superior——"

"I thought he was doing the superior patronizing, myself." He grinned at her amiably. "And personally, I don't give a damn about what he said to de Gaulle. And as for how close the bomb missed him in the viceroy's swimming pool——"

"That's what I mean," Laurel said. "You don't care what happens to anybody but yourself. If you people had been halfway decent to him, we wouldn't have had this sort of thing."

She bent down and picked up a handful of the discarded papers on the floor, thrust them into Monk Whitney's hand and stood watching him as he read them aloud. The first paragraph Myron had written over half a dozen times. The version he'd got farthest along with said:

Like most people who deal successfully with other people's domestic and parental relations in problem form, Judge Whitney has been unsuccessful in his own, sometimes to the point of melodrama. He and his sister, who lives next door to him in Rittenhouse Square, have not spoken to each other for some eight years. His children have been a steady disappointment. His batting average on them was fattened, however, when the war gave his son Monk—short for Monckton—an outlet for energies admirably adapted to the South Pacific, but not to the staid moribundity of the Quaker City. His——

Myron had crumpled up the sheet at that point. The next one was on the same general tack:

While not obtrusive or vulgar about it, the judge is nevertheless aware of the eminent fitness of the fate that arranged for him to be born in Philadelphia and a Whitney. His daughter's marriage to a man who as a boy carried his father's lunch in a tin box to the coal mine was a breach, never entirely healed by the fact that his son-in-law can write a check for the judge's gross earnings over a lifetime of serious legal and juristic effort without dipping into his current income enough to notice it. In the ordinary course of events in Philadelphia, Elsie Whitney might have been—and apparently was—expected to marry the socially acceptable son of a close friend of the family. The judge's present secretary was the unwitting cause of the tragedy that put an end to that, as the young man took over his father's financial obligations, and in so doing obligated the beautiful young secretary to the point that a movie finish is expected any——

That was as far as Myron had got with that one. Monk Whitney stood looking down at it steadily for a moment after he'd finished reading it. Then he crumpled it up with the others and tossed them back into Myron's wastebasket. He turned to Laurel with a sardonic grin.

"Being nice to Kane didn't net you much, Miss Frazier. You are marrying the young man, aren't you?"

The two red spots I'd seen in her cheeks at the Broad Street Station were burning there again.

"I certainly am."

He looked at her silently for an instant, the grin disappearing slowly. "You know, I wouldn't, if I were you."

Her eyes widened with astonishment. I thought as much at the sudden change in his tone as at what he'd said.

"You've never been in love with the guy," he added.

"I suppose you think I'm being grateful too?"

"As a matter of fact, it wasn't you I was thinking about. It's Travis. He's too good a guy——"

"You mean he's not in love with me? He's just marrying me because——" She stopped, her eyes incredulous, her breath coming quickly.

25

"I think you're both all mixed up with a lot of feeling grateful and sorry and this is what's expected of you, and neither of you has ever been in love with anybody." He stopped short, looking at her. "I guess I ought to keep my trap shut. I'm sorry, Laurel. I didn't——"

"You just don't know what you're talking about, that's all," she said quickly.

The words were blurred and scarcely audible as she made an abrupt move toward the door and was gone down the stairs.

Monk Whitney stood staring after her for an instant. He turned back slowly and looked at me. "I guess we're all wet," he said. "She is in love with the guy, after all."

He went on looking at me, so I said, probably acidly, "It looks like it. And what are you trying to do?"

He looked for an instant then as if he thought it was none of my business, which, heaven knows, was true. But he said curtly, "Aunt Abby's worried. She doesn't think Laurel's in love with Travis, or Travis with her, and Laurel'd marry Kane if she had an out. She asked me to talk to her—and now, because she didn't know she was up here. I came up to see if Kane was in. I guess I wasn't——"

I drew a deep breath. "Look," I said. "You talk about your aunt as if she were God. She's not. She's a scheming, worldly old woman, a lot smarter than all the rest of you put together."

I was more than a little annoyed, for some reason, or I expect I'd have used more tact.

"She knows perfectly well Laurel Frazier isn't in love with Myron Kane, but she's perfectly willing to sell her down the river just to stop him from writing that profile or to get back that document, whatever it is—one or both. I'll be willing to bet anything she and Myron have made a deal. She wrote me yesterday and said Laurel ought to be terribly grateful to Travis Elliot and she thought they'd be married soon. Now she's made a complete about-face. She's counting on all of you to make Laurel so unhappy she'll marry Myron. If that doesn't work, she'll probably put it to her, on the grounds that it'll save your father, because she knows the girl adores him and thinks this is all her fault. And if I were you, I'd be ashamed to have any part in it."

I stopped, rather appalled at my own temerity, and also startled at the towering structure I'd built up on the patch of quicksand of fact I'd overheard in the Broad Street Station.

"Well, of course I may be entirely wrong," I added hastily. "I haven't—I mean I guess I said that because I think you're being a little rough on her."

He stood there silently, thinking it over. "I wonder," he said. "Could be." He looked around the room. "Did she do all this?"

He indicated the hastily pushed-in drawers and littered papers. I nodded. He went around methodically straightening things up, still pretty sober-faced, picked up one or two of Myron's unfinished paragraphs lying on the floor, glanced at them and dropped them into the wastebasket.

"You think she's really in love with Travis?" he asked, looking at me. "And don't get me wrong, lady." His grin completely changed his whole face. "When I fall in love it's going to be with a gentle cow creature, so there'll be peace in the home. And Travis is my best friend. I just wondered, that's all."

"I wouldn't know, really," I said. "I never saw her till today."

"You never saw Aunt Abby till today, either, did you?"

We both laughed, and then we looked quickly at each other. Myron Kane was coming in. I could hear his voice booming up the stair well as he tried to make the old butler hear it was a nasty day out. It was, and not a lot better in, I thought as I hurried along to my room in the front and Monk Whitney went down the stairs. I could see him in the mirror there, going into his aunt's room. In a minute, I heard Myron whistling as he came up, and the door of his room close. It opened again shortly, and I waited about ten minutes before I followed him downstairs.

4

Mrs. Whitney and Myron were in her room. I could see her in the mirror just inside the door, but not him. She must have given him some signal, because his voice rose suddenly, expansively anecdotal with something about an Eastern ambassador. ". . . and I said, 'Effendi——' "

He stopped so abruptly, seeing me, that I saw while he knew someone was coming he didn't know it was to be his unwitting sponsor in the house. And it must have taken him all of a second to rally himself.

"Why, Gracie!" he exclaimed cordially, and I hate to be called "Gracie." "How very nice!"

He came toward me and gave me an affectionate kiss on the cheek. I hadn't, I guess, realized what close friends we were, and I don't think Mrs. Whitney was fooled either.

"Yes, isn't it Pleasant?" she said. "And didn't you bring a Letter for our Friend, Dear Child?"

"Yes, I did," I said. I'd forgotten it entirely in the press of interim business. I went over to the table where I'd left it with my bag when she'd dismissed Travis Elliot and me so peremptorily. "It's from a fan; he thinks you're divine."

I picked up my bag, but Mr. Toplady's letter wasn't under it. I looked inside. It wasn't there either.

"That's very funny," I said. "I thought I left it here."

I knew I had, in fact.

"It must be Somewhere, Dear Child," Mrs. Whitney said, without concern. "Or did you take it upstairs?"

I shook my head.

"Oh, well," Myron said.

It was spoken as by a public favorite to whom another fan letter was as a drop to the ocean, a grain to the desert. He'd returned to the mantel and was standing there with his elbow on it, at ease with himself and the world.

"It was from Someone who wrote a Book, Dear Boy," Mrs. Whitney said.

"No," I said. "It was from a little man named Albert Top-lady. I met him in a——"

I stopped, staring at him. It was unbelievable. He looked as if an invisible hand had landed him a paralyzing blow in the pit of the stomach. His face just in a fraction of an instant had turned a sickly gray-green, his mouth sagged open stupidly and there were beads of perspiration on his forehead and upper lip.

"Where is it? The letter!" he said.

His voice shook, and his body swayed as he took a step toward me. I thought he was going to grab the bag out of my hand and go through it himself.

"Grace, you've got to give it to me! Where is it?"

I stared at Mrs. Whitney, completely bewildered. She was resting back very calmly on her cushions, concentrating on Something Else, I supposed.

"I don't know where it is, Myron," I said. "It isn't here where I left it. Maybe one of the others picked it up by mistake."

"If they did," Abigail Whitney said placidly, "I'm sure they will return it, Dear Boy. They wouldn't open a sealed Letter addressed to anyone Else. It's one of the things that isn't Done."

A dark flush came into Myron's cheeks. "I wish you'd see if you took it upstairs, Grace," he said. He had made an effort to get himself under control, but his hands were still trembling and his voice harsh.

"Do, Dear Child," Mrs. Whitney said.

He followed me out of the room.

"Look, Myron," I said. "That letter was under my bag, and that's all I know about it. It is not upstairs."

The look in his face was as near despair as I've ever seen in all my life.

"My God, it'll ruin me," he whispered.

I'd have felt very sorry for him if I hadn't seen almost the same look in Laurel Frazier's eyes, and for much the same reason.

"It's sort of the biter bit, isn't it?" I said.

He stood there for a moment without answering, haggard and terribly diminished, someway. His mouth was trembling and there were actually tears in his eyes.

"Who was in there?" he demanded suddenly.

29

"Elsie and Sam Phelps, Monk Whitney, Travis Elliot, Mrs. Whitney and myself."

He nodded and went on up to his room.

I'd been standing facing him at the foot of the stairs. As I turned and started to go back into Mrs. Whitney's room, I stopped. I was looking directly into the mirrored panel at the right of the shell-ceilinged recess. The long mirror inside in her door was reflected in it. I could see her lying back on her cushions, staring thoughtfully up at the ceiling. I could not only see her, I could see a series of other reflections from other mirrors, and in them the lower hall—the hall I was in—and a part of the upper hall too. Those mirrors weren't just decorative detail in a modern interior architecture at all. They were placed, like the ones outside her window, with method and purpose. She could sit in her Empire swan-sleigh bed and see all approaches to her room. More than that, she could have seen Laurel Frazier go up to Myron's room, and seen that Myron hadn't either come in or gone up. Her sending Monk up, knowing Laurel was there, must have been a conscious and deliberate act.

The rattle and clack and ring of Myron's typewriter starting up at full speed came abruptly down the stair well. I saw Mrs. Whitney move, and I went on into her room.

"Did you find Myron's letter?" she asked, more to be polite than anything else, from her manner.

"No. What happened to it?" I asked, meeting her blue gaze directly.

"It's so difficult to be Sure about things, isn't it?" she said vaguely.

"Didn't you see who took it?"

"I've got awfully blind with Advancing Years," she said. "But you've got eyes, Dear Child. You should train yourself to use them."

It could have meant a lot of things. At the moment, I would have bet anything she had it stowed away somewhere under her cushions.

"And there's something else," she said. "I heard you tell my Nephew I was a scheming, Worldly Old Woman."

I was so taken aback that I wasn't sure whether she said, "I heard you tell" or "I hear you told." If it was the first, she must have had very keen ears, because I couldn't now hear the sound of Myron's typewriter. If the other, it meant, of course, that Monk had repeated it to her. I'd have thought better of him, but, after all, I had no way of knowing what he would do.

She was looking at me with a faintly amused gleam in her old blue eyes.

"Well," I began, by way of apology.

"Not at all, Dear Child, not At All," she said promptly. "I thought it was very Intelligent in you, and not Unworldly in itself. My nephew would never have thought of it. But you will understand I won't need your Policeman now. Their methods are tedious and long-drawn-out; I'm sure my Own are better." She looked past me at the mirror beside the door. "Myron is going out. I thought he was Most Disturbed, didn't you?"

I was finding it rapidly more difficult to think at all. I was appalled. I just stood there staring at her, blankly.

"Don't be Naïve, Dear Child," she said. "What I have suggested is the Best Possible Solution for everybody."

"For everybody except Laurel Frazier," I said, with some warmth.

"For Everybody," she repeated. "If Laurel marries Travis, she'll be buried alive out on the Main Line. She'll take him to the eight-thirty train every morning, and meet him again at five-thirty. She'll take the children to school, and she'll pick them up. She'll play tennis and bridge and go to Meetings, and in five years she'll be just like Elsie Phelps, a typical suburban matron. It is a Living Death. If she marries Myron Kane, she'll live in New York and Washington and abroad. Laurel is perfectly aware the only thing wrong with Myron Kane is a sense of Social Inferiority. Her background is excellent Philadelphia, all Myron Kane needs to make a Powerful Person of him. He needs her, Travis does not. Any nice girl, preferably one not so bright as Laurel is, is all dear Travis needs."

"It doesn't matter whether she's in love with Myron or not, I take it," I said, as calmly as I could.

Her hands moved slightly on the green cover. "Love has very little to do with marriage, in my opinion, and I've had sufficient Experience to speak with Authority. Actually, the nearest to love Laurel has ever come is her Blind Hero Worship for my Brother. She was attracted to Myron in London. Money, I think, has more to do with marriage than Love has, and I'm prepared to underwrite that aspect of Myron and Laurel's life, even though he has a handsome income of his own from his Writings."

31

"Why," I asked, "don't you just buy him off, and leave Laurel out of the picture?"

She looked at me placidly for an instant, and when she spoke, Colonel Primrose himself couldn't have been more suave. "The Dear Boy can't be bought with money. I would have failed if I had attempted anything as unpolitic as that. I have a very simple Code of Ethics, Dear Child. I believe a single Mistake, however Serious, should not be held against a man who has Repented it and become a Respected Citizen. I think the Dead Past should be allowed to stay Buried."

Her voice was firm and clear, and the only sign of agitation was her hand fiddling with the dial of the small radio on the table beside her.

"I am sure Elsie is right in saying that if it had not been that Laurel and Myron Kane were attracted to each other in London last summer, he would never have come here to write a Profile of my Brother. He would not have had the opportunity to dig up the Past. If by marrying him, Laurel can undo the Harm she has done—however much my Brother would pretend to be opposed to it—I feel she should do it. But I would be the Last to attempt to Force her to do it or even allow her to know I thought it her Duty."

What she called everything she'd been saying up to that point, I had no idea.

"You ask me very legitimately, I think, what there can be in my Brother's life that cannot be published in *The Saturday Evening Post*," she went on. "You have never met my Brother?"

I shook my head.

"They complain that dear Monk Whitney is wild and untractable, and had to have a War to Come of Age," she said. "My brother didn't have a War, and his son is a pale and docile Lamb compared with him. Women adored him. He married, because it was expected of him, the way his son will no doubt do—before he met the woman he adored. He paid for that, and so did she. That is what Elsie wants kept out of *The Saturday Evening Post*."

She stopped for a moment, looking very steadily at me. "It is not what I want kept out. My Brother killed a man. That is what I want kept out. That is why I don't see my Brother. He doesn't know I know it. That man is dead. I loved him, but I want him to stay dead. I don't want another Useful Life destroyed because of one Mistake."

Her voice was vibrating, her eyes a burning vivid blue

32

under the preposterous fuzz of henna hair. I'd hardly noticed that she had dropped all but the emphasis of her usual round-about speech, and all her vagueness.

"That, Dear Child, is why I would be happy to see Laurel marry Myron Kane," she said. "And now, I'm Very Tired. Will you close the door as you go out? One can't always be sure, my dear. We may still need your Policeman."

I was too torn by conflicting ideas and emotions and too bewildered by the whole thing to think very clearly or even think at all. I pulled the door shut behind me and stood there for a moment, my hand still on the knob. Then I sort of came to, and blinked my eyes without quite believing I was seeing properly.

The girl with the copper hair and the wood-hyacinth eyes was sitting as motionless and white as marble in the needle-point armchair beside the shell-ceilinged recess. Mrs. Whitney had not been talking to me. Every word she'd said she'd said to Laurel Frazier.

5

The girl sat there in the armchair in front of the shell-ceilinged recess, motionless and white as alabaster, shocked and completely stunned. And I was nearly as much so myself, at what Abigail Whitney had done, and at what she wanted kept out of *The Saturday Evening Post*. "My Brother killed a man." If those words were still going crazily around in my mind, however, they must have been infinitely more intense and paralyzing in Laurel Frazier's. I thought back, trying to decide how much she could have heard, at what point Mrs. Whitney had known she was there and couldn't help but hear. It must have been when she'd stopped and then said that about the dead past burying its dead, not coming back to destroy a useful citizen. That, of course, must have been for Laurel, for up to then she had certainly never referred to her brother in terms like that.

And when she'd said to me, "You ask me very legitimately, I think, what there can be in my Brother's life that cannot be published in *The Saturday Evening Post*," I knew she was talking to Laurel Frazier—because I hadn't asked her at all. And, of course, when she'd said it was Laurel's duty to undo the harm she'd done, but that her brother would pretend to oppose it and she'd be the last to try to force it, every word she'd said had been deliberately phrased and timed, and I'd been nothing at all but the simplest means to an end.

I looked at the girl, trying to think of something to say, but there wasn't anything. She raised her hand slowly and moved it across her forehead as if trying to wipe everything away. Then she got up and walked mechanically across the hall into the library at the back. I followed her after a moment. A small table was set in front of the fire, laid for one and glistening with damask and silver.

34

She turned to me. "This is for you," she said slowly, out of a sort of thick fog. "Eat something, will you? I'll wait. I want you to go with me. Please. I want to think."

As she stood in front of the fire, looking down into it, the tawny brilliance of her hair made the flames look a pallid yellow and without much warmth.

"Are you going to tell him?" she asked after a few minutes.

"Tell who?"

"Your policeman. Colonel Primrose. Isn't he the detective she had you bring up? Myron said you were his—his assistant."

I caught my breath and tried not to choke. "Myron," I said, "is crazy. Colonel Primrose isn't an ordinary detective in the first place, and I'm anything but his assistant in the second. Furthermore, I didn't bring him up, because he's already here. And I haven't thought about telling him or not telling him. It was as much of a—a shock to me as it was to you."

She shook her head mechanically. "You don't know him— the judge, I mean. He's wonderful. But he's a——" She stopped and began again after a moment. "I could believe he'd kill a man. I saw him angry once. But——" She hesitated again, and went on. "About this . . . woman she was talking about. I don't think Myron knows that. And the judge wouldn't mind anyway. He loved her very deeply. He tried every way there was to marry her. He's not ashamed of it. It's just that Elsie doesn't understand. Of course she wouldn't. If that came out in *The Saturday Evening Post*, he wouldn't mind at all, because no story of his life would be true without her. His friends all knew it. It was when Elsie and Sam came and dared to talk about disgrace that I saw him angry."

"But of course that's not the kind of thing they'd want to print, anyway," I said.

She looked at me for an instant and changed the subject entirely. "That's not what we're talking about, is it? It's the other thing we've got to stop—even if I have to marry Myron Kane to stop it."

She stood looking down, lost in the dancing movement of the flames along the oak logs.

"And I would marry him, if it was the only way out," she said slowly, at last. "I'd hate him for it. But what she said is

35

right. It is my fault. But I'd have to know it was the only way. So, if you're ready, I'd like you to go with me to see Travis."

"Travis?" I asked. I would have thought Judge Whitney was the person to see, and I said so.

"Do you think I'd dare go and tell him I'd heard he killed somebody? I wouldn't want him ever to know I knew, in the first place. And he'd die before he'd let me marry somebody to save him anything. You don't know him. Travis is a first-rate lawyer, and he adores the judge. Maybe he'll—— Oh, I just don't know. It's just that he and I are the ones that owe him the most—more than Elsie or Monk, really."

I couldn't think of anything at all to say.

"So if you're ready, I wish you'd go with me. Now that you know, too, and you're a friend of Myron's. Maybe there's something we can do."

I was more than a little dubious about it, especially at being on a basis of friendship with Myron, but I went upstairs, got my coat and galoshes and came down again. She was waiting for me in the lower hall, standing by the door, her forehead pressed against the glass to cool what must have been a throbbing ache inside it.

The sleet had almost stopped, but it was bitterly cold with the wind whipping through the naked branches of the buttonwood trees in the square, and the sidewalks like glass underfoot. We cut across the corner of the square into 19th Street again and went along across Spruce to Delancey Place, and turned right. It was like walking into a different period, with the old gaslights shimmering under the trees that lined each side of the narrow, empty street. It had escaped the blight fallen on the others around it, as it jogged in and out at angles useless for streetcars and inconvenient for any traffic, and the brownstone and brick houses had a remote and quiet dignity retained from a lost older day.

We'd gone about halfway along the block, silent since we'd left the square, when Laurel touched my arm and stopped abruptly.

"Look," she said.

A man had come hurriedly down the steps of a house a little farther along. As she spoke, his feet shot out from under him on the icy steps and he landed at the bottom, catching himself grotesquely on the railing, his stick flying out of his hand and his hat rolling to the curb. He picked himself up quickly, retrieved his hat and cane, started our way, I thought, then turned and went rapidly off in the other. It was Myron Kane.

"That's Travis' house," Laurel said. "What do you suppose——"

She stopped, her hand closing on my arm sharply.

A man had disengaged himself from the shadow of the tree on the other side of the street and was crossing over. He came into the perimeter of light in front of Travis Elliot's house, stepped up onto the curb and stood there waiting for us.

"What are you two gals doing here?" he asked. It wasn't till then that I recognized Monk Whitney.

"What are you doing out of uniform?" Laurel retorted.

"I'm not on business befitting an officer and a gentleman, Coppertop," he said calmly. "Let's say I'm exercising, which makes it okay. I still don't know what you're doing."

He lighted a cigarette, his eyes searching hers intently across the tip of flame from his lighter.

"We're going to see Travis," she said. "Don't let us keep you, major."

"I figured that one out already, and you're not keeping me. In fact, I'm coming along."

She stood there stiffly for an instant, and then we followed him up the steps. There was a sharp click-click-click as he pressed the bell. He opened the door and stood aside as we went in. It was a handsome house of the late 1890 taste, and had the air of needing a woman's hand and a couple of open windows. The dark green walls were covered with large lithographs and heavy gilt-framed pictures of cows standing placidly around in fields by brooks. Upstairs, the back library, where Travis Elliot was, was slightly more modern. The portraits of past Elliots looked down from the walls and a coal fire burned in the grate. Travis Elliot himself looked a little grim, I thought, as we came in. He gave Monk's civilian clothes a surprised glance as he helped Laurel with her coat. It was the first time I'd seen him with her, and if they were in love with each other, they were certainly matter-of-fact about it, I thought. They seemed much more like brother and sister to me.

"We saw Kane coming out," Monk said. "What did he want?"

Travis Elliot opened the cellarette at the end of the long sofa by the library table.

"The affairs of a client are a sacred trust," he said easily. "I

37

couldn't possibly discuss them with you. Did you take the letter Mrs. Latham brought him, by the way?"

"Not me," Monk said. "I've got my own fan mail to answer. Somebody take it?"

"Somebody took it. And made a systematic search of his room to boot—or so he says. It's apparently wrong to meddle with private papers if they belong to Myron Kane."

Travis Elliot turned to me. "Sure you left it in Aunt Abby's room, Mrs. Latham?"

I nodded. "Yes, I am."

Laurel was listening, looking from one of us to the other. "Who did take it?" she asked abruptly. "And what was it?"

Travis shook his head. "I gather it wasn't a fan letter. He wouldn't say what it was, except that he damn well wants it back quick. He's in a cold sweat about it. I asked him how I thought I could get it back if he won't tell me what it is or who wrote it. Who did you say gave it to you, Mrs. Latham?"

I started to say, "Albert Toplady," and caught a swift glance from Monk.

"I've forgotten, I'm afraid," I said.

Monk set his glass of whisky and soda on the mantel. "The only other people who could have taken it," he said, very casually, "were Elsie and Soapy Sam."

Travis nodded. "And Sam wouldn't. That leaves Elsie. She'd take it if she thought there was anything in it and got the chance. She'd think it was her duty. But why should she think there was anything in it? And I wasn't paying any attention to either of them." He looked at Monk. "I think," he said coolly, "that if we could get that letter—whatever it is—we'd have Kane just where we want him. There's something about it—— He offered, just now, to turn over his manuscript and give back any other papers he's got, if he gets that letter, unopened, before he leaves for New York tomorrow. If he doesn't——" He picked up the poker and stirred the fire.

"If he doesn't, what?" Laurel asked.

"He's going to keep a dinner date, he says, with the head of the bar association. The district attorney will be there."

A coal dropped out of the fire and clattered noisily on the brick hearth, and at the same moment the bell pealed loudly out in the hall. Monk Whitney was watching Laurel intently. She was standing taut and motionless, her whole bearing a dead giveaway that Myron's hardly veiled threat had meaning to her that it did not have to him or Travis.

Travis went over to the switch and pressed the button. The front door opened.

"Travis?" A full deep voice I hadn't heard before came up the stairway. Laurel took a deep breath and looked urgently at Monk. I saw his jaw tense as he turned and stood looking down into the fire. I thought he was more disturbed than he had been at any time before.

Travis had gone out into the hall.

"Come on up, sir," he was saying, and I could hear a muffled pattern of more than one pair of feet on the carpeted stairs. "Oh, hello, Sam."

There was a good deal less cordiality in his greeting then than when he'd spoken first. Sam Phelps, I thought, in spite of how much Myron Kane thought he could write a check for, was certainly not what one might call a universal favorite. It was Judge Whitney, however, not Sam, that I was interested in, and when he came up into the room, I could see why Laurel Frazier thought about him as she did. He was large and robust, with thick white hair and shaggy, grizzled eyebrows over a pair of very wise blue eyes. His face was broad, shaped like his son's, but filled out and mature. It was strong as iron, full of repose and understanding.

"This is Mrs. Latham, judge," Travis said. He followed him in, leaving Sam Phelps to bring up the rear.

Judge Whitney took my hand in a warm, friendly grasp. "How do you do, Mrs. Latham? I dined with your friend Colonel Primrose this evening. He said you're staying with my sister Abigail. I hope that isn't going to keep me from having the pleasure of seeing you." The twinkle in his eye disappeared as he turned. "You've met my daughter's husband, Mr. Phelps, I believe?"

Sam Phelps and I murmured something at each other. Judge Whitney went over to the fireplace.

"I've come after the letter that Mrs. Latham brought to Myron Kane," he said calmly.

"We were just talking about it, sir," Travis said.

"I presumed as much. Which of you has it?"

Monk moved over by me. "Better hand it out, Sambo," he said.

Sam Phelps' polished dome flushed. "You're just trying to annoy me, Monk," he said angrily. "The first I knew of it was when Kane called me from here an hour ago. I reported it to the judge at once. I'm not in a position to——"

"I don't doubt you have the best intentions in the world—one or all of you," Judge Whitney said. It was almost as if he had been concentrating on Something Else, too, and was unaware his son-in-law was speaking. "Let me say you are badly advised. It's of the utmost importance that that letter be returned to Myron Kane—and immediately."

He stopped as if waiting for someone to hand it over. When no one moved or spoke, he settled back in his chair.

"I appreciate your motive in all this," he said patiently. "I don't appreciate the attitude you all seem to take that I must be protected, against myself or against Kane." A faint smile flickered for an instant in his eyes. "I can only tell you that this letter will make matters infinitely worse. It will do irreparable harm, and no good whatsoever. It won't get the manuscript for you, because it's already in. Kane delivered it to the *Post* some time ago."

There was a suspended silence in the room when he stopped. No one looked at Travis, who'd been so sure the letter was all that was needed to stop Myron Kane's article from ever going to the *Post* or to get back the document Laurel had given him in the judge's file.

"I may also say that blackmail, in any form, is never justifiable," Judge Whitney said quietly. "That letter belongs to Kane. It was taken by some one of you at my sister's house this evening."

He turned to his son. "Have you got it, Monk?"

"No, sir," Monk said. "I have not."

"Travis?"

"No, sir."

"Laurel?"

"I didn't know about it, even, till a few minutes ago, sir."

He looked at me. I shook my head.

Laurel spoke calmly. "What about Elsie? Has anyone asked her?"

"Don't be ridiculous," Sam said sharply. "Of course I haven't asked her."

"Why don't you phone and do it now?"

"She's not at home; she's at a meeting. I'm sure she would have told me——"

Judge Whitney rose. "I am disappointed," he said quietly. "I won't believe one of you would have deliberately told me a falsehood, from whatever motive, until I'm forced to do so.

. . . Have Elsie phone me as soon as she gets home, Sam." He turned back at the door. "I beg you, as earnestly as I know how," he said, "to believe me when I say that whoever has that letter of Myron Kane's is doing a wantonly cruel and inhuman thing. I feel that very intensely and very personally. I want it returned to me tonight. I'll wait up for it. Good night to all of you."

Nobody moved, even to help him on with his coat. He went slowly down the stairs, the door closed behind him.

"You've got that letter, Monk," Sam Phelps said abruptly.

Monk Whitney grinned. "Why don't you go, Sam?" he asked. "Why don't you and Elsie take a trip to the Argentine? Why don't you leave tonight, before we all disgrace you?"

Sam flushed, started to say something, changed his mind, nodded curtly to us and went out.

Laurel looked at Monk. Her face was quite pale. "You have got it, Monk. I don't see how you can lie to him!"

He was looking at her, one eyebrow raised sardonically, and turned at Travis Elliot's triumphant exclamation, "Toplady! That's the fellow's name! I knew I'd——"

"Then forget it," Monk said curtly. He strode over and picked up my coat. "Coming?"

Laurel took a step forward. "Where are you going?"

"That's my business, Coppertop."

He was holding my coat out to me.

She looked at him for an instant, turned quickly, picked up the telephone at the end of the library table and spun the dial around swiftly.

"Who are you calling?"

"That's my business!" Laurel said hotly, "But if you want to know, I'm calling Myron Kane! There's one way to settle this, and if I have to marry him to get that——"

He was across the room in two swift strides, jerked the telephone out of her hand and slammed it down on the cradle.

"No, you're not," he said quietly. "We don't need a woman to save our necks."

They stood there facing each other, both of them furious, leaving Travis Elliot and myself practically stupefied. He turned suddenly and came back, stopping at the door.

"If you want to marry Kane, Coppertop, that's your business . . . and Trav's. But don't pull that martyr stuff on us. . . . Are you ready, Mrs. Latham?"

6

He slammed the front door shut and struggled into his overcoat.

"Careful of the ice," he said shortly.

At the bottom of the steps, he stopped, looking at me oddly.

"My God," he said, with a kind of suppressed groan, "you'd think I gave a damn who she married, wouldn't you? Well, I don't. Just so she doesn't do it thinking she's Joan of Arc."

He took my arm and steered me along the slippery sidewalk.

"Look," he said. "Would you know what happens to manuscripts that go to the *Post*?"

We crossed the narrow opening of Manning Street toward the square.

"Well," I said, "the *Post*——"

"You don't need to tell me about the *Post*. I know all about that. I used to go on a tour through the plant with a couple of hundred other kids every week. If you stacked one issue, it would be more than twenty-five times as high as the Empire State Building and the paper rolled out would reach more than ten times the distance from New York to Chicago. It takes over two hundred miles of wire to make staples to bind it and forty tons of ink a week and more than seventy presses running twenty-four hours a day to print it. Or that's what it used to be. I was going to be a printer once myself—like Benjamin Franklin. I even used to know the number of pieces of glass they baked to make that Maxfield Parrish Dream Garden in the lobby. But that's not what I mean. I mean, what happens to Myron's manuscript? Who's got it now? Where is it?"

"All I know is what Mark Childs told me when he did the profile of Colonel Primrose," I said. "He gave it to Bob Fuoss at lunchtime. Two of the associate editors—I think Jack Alexander was one of them—read it that afternoon, and Ben Hibbs took it home that night. He has to read everything that goes in the magazine. Ben Hibbs probably has this now. They read so fast, people glue pages together to make sure they read it all, they tell me."

"If Mr. Hibbs okays it tonight, what happens?"

"I suppose they might edit it in the morning and send it up to Composition right away," I said. "If it's timely. Or it might stay around a while. I don't know, really. Why?"

"I just wondered. If Elsie and Sam hadn't chucked their weight about so, I'd go and talk to Hibbs in the morning. As a matter of fact, I guess I'll just go now."

"He lives out on the Main Line," I said. "They say he's very nice, but he has one curious eccentricity. He goes to bed at night. It's a grass-root habit that he picked up as a child in Kansas. He's supposed to be mild, but I believe that's at nine-thirty in the morning."

"Okay, Dear Child," he said imperturbably. "I get it."

We were cutting across the jog in 19th Street to Mrs. Whitney's house. The lights were still on in her room, and in the windows in her brother's house next door. It seemed incredible to think they'd lived so close to each other and yet been so remote for so many years.

"You know," I said, "I wish somebody would ask me what I think about all this."

"Okay. What?"

"I think you're a lot of dopes. Now that I've met your father, I don't believe for one instant that Myron Kane would have the courage to offend him, even if he wanted to. I think everything in that profile is there with your father's knowledge and consent. At least everything about himself. Myron might take pot shots at you and Elsie and Sam, but that won't hurt anybody. You know the business about present fears being less than horrible imaginings."

He didn't say anything until we'd reached his aunt's doorway. "It's funny, you know, Grace," he said then, "but I never realized till I was out there that I must have been an awful pain in the neck to him. Or how much I—well, I guess worshiped him is what I mean." He looked at me and grinned suddenly. "I guess it's a little too much below

43

freezing to make you stand out here and listen to the story of my life," he said. "What I mean is, if I could save him a half second's worry——"

"You could give him Myron Kane's letter," I said.

His jaw hardened. He stood there silently.

"And look. You don't seriously think your father ever—— I mean, that there's anything in his life—— He seems so——" I hesitated, and so did he.

"He wasn't always as judicial as he is now," he said then. "Well, anyhow, good night. I'll see you tomorrow. Wait, I'll let you in; I've got a key. I guess I'll go up and say good night to the old gal. Quiet; she may be asleep."

The grilled door moved noiselessly and we slipped in onto the thick beige carpet of the dimly lit lower hall. We started up the curving marble staircase. He gripped my arm suddenly, almost throwing me off balance. I caught myself, staring at him. He was standing there, rigid and motionless, his eyes fixed in a kind of incredulous, thunderstruck amazement on the mirrored panel in the wall.

In it was an oblong of light, brilliant in the dim glow of the hall. I could see Abigail Whitney. She was talking to her brother. Judge Whitney stood there, his head bowed a little. The unbelievable thing was that she was standing too. Her face was half turned from us, her back was straight as an arrow, and she moved back and forth, not even a cane in her hand, as able to walk as Monk or I. Her voice was clear as a bell in the silent house, and vibrant with intensity.

"You killed Douglas Elliot, Nathaniel. There's no use trying to evade it. The document Laurel gave Myron Kane—— "

Monk Whitney caught my arm in a tighter hold and drew me out of the focus of the mirror and down the stairs. The blood was beating in my ears; I couldn't have heard any more, even if anyone had needed to hear more. We got outside. He stood holding the doorknob, letting it slip softly to. Then he leaned unsteadily for a moment against the stone frame, his face quite white. It seemed from ages to infinity before either of us moved, and then we just looked at each other.

"I can't ask you not to say anything," he said. The words were twisted and tortured.

"Oh, I won't," I whispered. "I promise I won't, ever."

He held out his hand and grasped mine. Then he turned and pressed the doorbell. He was gone when the butler came.

I hadn't even seen him go. He'd gone as quickly and as quietly as if he'd been slipping through some South Pacific jungle.

I went upstairs slowly. It was as quiet as the grave. Mrs. Whitney's door was open and her lights were on. I could see her lying on the yellow cushions, her bright sharp eyes watching me intently in the mirror.

"Come in, Dear Child," she called as I passed the door.

I think it was the hardest thing I ever did in my life. I don't think I'll ever have anything so hard to do again. I rubbed my face with my hands to get a little color back, steadied my shaking knees and went in.

"Where on Earth have you Been, Dear Child? I was Alarmed about you. Your Policeman telephoned three times. But don't tell me now, I am very Tired. Good night. Dear Myron isn't in yet Either. You keep such odd hours in Washington, Dear Child."

I got out and went upstairs. I hadn't seen Judge Whitney. It seemed odd to think of his hiding in a closet somewhere, waiting for me to close my door, so he could slip out and home. It was more than odd, it was ghastly, and so was the whole thing. I shut my door and sat down on the side of the bed. I couldn't stop shaking enough to get my coat off, and for hours after I got into bed I lay there, freezing and unable to get warm.

Why had Abigail Whitney pretended for all those years that she was bedridden? What had kept her there, lying all day on her yellow cushions, watching in her mirrors, getting up at night, so her muscles wouldn't atrophy, and—who could tell?—perhaps even slipping out and wandering alone in the empty darkness of the square?

I lay there listening. Myron Kane still hadn't come in. I wondered where he could have gone, and then I wondered what could be in the letter Albert Toplady had given me in the taxi that was ruinous enough for Myron to be willing to barter the knowledge he had of Judge Whitney for it. And incredible as it must seem, it struck me then, for the first time, that the reason Myron had gone to Travis Elliot was not that Travis was a lawyer, but that he was the son of the man Judge Whitney had killed. And Travis Elliot didn't know it. Myron hadn't told him what he was going to see the district attorney for. I was sure of that. If he had, Travis could never have received Judge Whitney as warmly as he had done—not in his father's own house, not so soon after he

45

had learned anything so ghastly. It seemed suddenly to take on a kind of tragic irony. They were all appealing to Travis to help them protect his father's murderer. And Judge Whitney's demand that Albert Toplady's letter to Myron be returned to him—he'd wait up for it, he'd said—had a new and astonishing significance. It was not to save Myron, as I'd thought it was, that he'd come. It was to save himself. "A Useful Life," Abigail Whitney had said. "Let the Dead Past stay Buried."

In the shadowy silence of the room, it seemed to me in some way, bewildered as I was, to begin to fit together and make sense. If I could only see Colonel Primrose, I thought, and then I remembered. I'd promised Monk, and though I'd never been very good at keeping knowledge from Colonel Primrose, this was different. If I could tell him, he might be able to help, but I knew he wouldn't. Behind the urbane humor with which he regards human frailty, I knew there was a rigid and uncompromising sense of justice and honor that neither friendship nor affection would make him deviate from by a hair's breadth. I knew perfectly well that if the occasion rose he would hang both me and Sergeant Buck to the nearing sycamore tree without batting more than half an eye.

I was so absorbed in what seemed to me the issuing of some kind of clarity out of everything, and in my determination to keep one secret in my life, that I'd finally got warm without knowing it. I looked at my traveling watch on the table. It was almost three o'clock. I got up reluctantly to open a window to let in a little air, and stood for a moment looking out. Seeing other buildings and lighted streets brought a sense of some kind of perspective to my distracted mind. Abigail Whitney, even if she was at this moment moving stealthily about the house, wasn't so terrifying when I was looking out on a sleeping world where other people were sane and normal.

I put my hand out to lift the sash and stopped. A dark figure was coming rapidly across the square, zigzagging a course over the intercepting paths that led toward 19th Street. There was something familiar about it, which is why I stood watching until it got to the curb and started across the street. It was Monk Whitney. Even in the shadowy darkness I recognized him, before I saw him head for his father's house next door. I opened the window after a moment and went back to bed, and for several minutes I kept a disturbing after-image of a man moving quickly, not just coming home, but coming home from something.

And next morning at nine-thirty I didn't have much doubt about what it was. The deaf butler brought my breakfast, aided by a gaunt, stiffly starched maid as old or older, whose "The mistress wishes good morning to you, ma'am," was as thick and Irish as a peat bog. The butler went back into the hall and returned with an ivory-lacquered telephone that he plugged in beside the bed and handed me.

"It's a message for you, ma'am, it is," the woman said. She began picking up my clothes, left pretty much where I'd got out of them the night before.

I must be careful, I thought. I knew it was Colonel Primrose before I heard his voice, and the night before flashed vividly back, like life in a drowning man's memory: "I think the Dead Past should be allowed to stay Buried."

"Hello," he said. "I tried to get you last night. Have you heard the news?"

I thought it was the war he meant, but it wasn't.

"Ben Hibbs' house was broken into last night."

I caught my breath sharply and tried to cover the mouthpiece with my hand, but it was too late.

"What's the matter?" he asked.

"Nothing," I said. "You just made me spill some hot coffee." I could hardly hope it would deceive him. "I hope they didn't take much," I said. It sounded silly, but at least more natural than asking "Who?"

"Just his brief case, oddly enough," Colonel Primrose said. He was as placid as ever. "It was full of manuscripts he'd taken home to read last night. I just talked to him. They got in his study window, sometime around two. Some crank, apparently. A neighbor saw a car there."

I wanted to ask a dozen other questions, but I didn't dare. I knew from experience that the association of ideas in my mind would present no problem to him. And I was trying to remember if Monk Whitney had been carrying a brief case when he'd hurried across the street in the early hours of the morning.

"What about lunch?" he said. "I'm free unless the book-keeper from the Quaker Trust shows up later. He hasn't come in yet, and——"

I'd known, of course, that the association of ideas can work two ways, but before I could stop I heard, with repentant horror, my voice saying, "Not Mr. Albert Toplady, by any chance?"

There was the shortest silence at the other end.

"Yes," Colonel Primrose said, very affably. "How did you know?"

If thy right hand offend thee, cut it off, I thought; *if thy tongue offend thee, tear it out.* I would gladly have got rid of mine any way I could just then.

"We used to have an account there," I said lamely. "The name stuck, I guess."

"He's been there for years," Colonel Primrose said. "I'll pick you up at noon, then. I'm going over to Curtis to see Hibbs now."

I put down the phone and sat there unhappily, remembering Monk shaking his head at me when Travis was trying to remember who I'd said had given me the letter for Myron. And here I was, two minutes after I'd told myself I must be careful. It seems very strange to me, at this point, that it never so much as crossed my mind just then that there was anything odd in what Colonel Primrose had told me. That there might be any connection between Albert Toplady's not showing up at the bank that morning and the letter I'd failed to deliver for him, or Myron's not coming home the night before, just never occurred to me. I simply sat there, acutely unhappy about not keeping my mouth shut when Colonel Primrose called.

And that wasn't because I thought I'd done anything irreparable as much as it was a grim warning of what I could expect I'd say on the impulse of the moment sometime when Judge Whitney's name came up, or Abigail Whitney's—or Douglas Elliot's. I could already hear myself: "Oh, you mean Travis Elliot's father, the man Judge Whitney killed. And you know, the judge's sister Abigail isn't bedridden at all."

I decided then that Washington, D. C., was the place for me, where we have so many murders of our own that no one's interested in imported ones, and where if more people stayed at home pretending they were bedridden it would be wonderful.

But that was before I took a bath and dressed and met Myron Kane on the stairs coming up to his room. He looked awful. He had black circles under his eyes and he hadn't shaved. All the starched, immaculate grooming that made him look as if he were the combined London tailors' contribution to Allied amity was so gone that it was hard to believe he had on the same clothes he'd had on the day before.

"Come in here, Grace; I want to talk to you," he said peremptorily.

He closed the door of his room behind me and sat down on his bed without even taking off his overcoat. Then he got up, went to his typewriter, pulled out the piece of paper in it and looked at it.

"Somebody's been in here again, damn it," he said. He turned to me. "Look, Grace. I'm being persecuted around here."

When I said "Oh," my voice, I suppose, must have sounded a little like Charlie McCarthy's.

"I want to see Primrose. Where is he?"

"He's at the *Post*, I believe," I said. And when I went on, I knew what I was saying this time. "He was at the Quaker Trust Company, but your admirer, Mr. Toplady, didn't show. So he's free. I'm having lunch with him."

He looked at me sharply. I had the feeling he already knew about that or at least knew why Colonel Primrose was at the bank. He was speculating, I thought, as to whether I knew.

"I'm getting pretty sore," he said. "I'm getting out of here today. Let me tell you something. I happened across something that will knock somebody around here sky-west. I wasn't going to use it, but now I am going to. Nobody's treating me like dirt. I'm a lot smarter than these people are, and I can hurt them worse than they can hurt me."

"Myron," I said, "why don't you give back that—document, whatever it is, that you've got, and let them give you back your letter, and call it off?"

He looked at me intently again. "They don't need proof to ruin me," he said curtly. "I need proof. And I'm keeping it—for a while—even if I do get my letter."

"But your manuscript? You've turned that in to the *Post*, haven't you?"

He nodded. "Some days ago, in fact. I didn't tell them that. But I'm getting it back today. I'll play ball if they will." He looked morosely around the room. "You can tell them they needn't go through my stuff any more. I'm not ass enough to leave anything here. And look, Grace. I want you to do something for me."

"No indeed," I said. I shook my head firmly. "I'm having no part in this, Myron."

49

"I'm not asking you to. I'll run this show myself. But I've sent some of my mail to your house. It's the only private Washington address I could remember. Will you hang on to it till I give you a forwarding address?"

"Myron," I said, "did you send that——"

"I sent a copy of my profile of Judge Whitney, because people here keep sticking their snoots into my stuff."

"Which you started, didn't you?"

He nodded coolly. "And am going to finish." Then he gave me an angry glare. "And I might have known whose side you'd be on. If you'll scram, I'd like to get a bath and pack." He opened the door for me. "And look. When you see Primrose, just shut up. I'll handle this business my own way."

I went out. Abigail Whitney's door was closed, which was just as well, I thought. Myron's voice was high-pitched and strident, and if she'd overheard me calling her a scheming, worldly old woman she couldn't very well have helped hearing his uncomplimentary allusion to her nose.

Her door hadn't opened and Myron hadn't come down when Colonel Primrose called for me shortly before noon. When I got down, he was waiting in the first-floor front room. It was a formal, rather lovely room in pale old-gold Louis Quinze and gray, but lifeless, as rooms are that are never used. Colonel Primrose was looking around it with more interest than he usually shows in interior decoration, his black eyes as alert as a terrier's by a rat hole.

"Well," I said, "Mrs. Whitney's changed her mind about you. She thought at first she wanted you to help her, but now she doesn't."

"I'm sorry," he said. "I'd like to meet her."

"She's an extraordinary woman." I could certainly say that much truthfully, I thought. "What about the Hibbs burglary?"

"His brief case was left at the Sansom Street entrance to the Curtis Building, sometime early this morning. Nothing gone. One of the watchmen found it. The police are fingerprinting it."

"Were there fingerprints at the house?"

He shook his head. "Footprints, but the sun's melted them. It was a big man. Can't tell you any more. Not a professional, but quiet."

I asked, as casually as I could, "Have they any idea what he was looking for?"

"Not the foggiest. They've run several pieces on some pretty shady setups, like the one Jack Alexander did on Atlantic City, but nothing like that's scheduled at the moment. Some crackpot, probably—though most of them make a personal call at the office. We'll go around after lunch and see if anything's happened."

I couldn't tell whether he was being honest or cagey, and I didn't dare try to find out. Then it occurred to me that obviously, if that manuscript of the profile of Judge Whitney had been in as long as Myron had said it had, it wouldn't have been among those in Ben Hibbs' brief case last night.

"What brought you up here?" he asked, as we were going down the front steps. "You seemed to be just a little incoherent over the telephone."

There's nothing military about Colonel Primrose's slightly rotund figure; he leaves all that to his sergeant. Except for the bullet wound in his neck that makes him cock his head down and around when he looks sideways, and his black eyes that contract like an old parrot's, the Army doesn't seem to have left many traces on him. I'm so accustomed to his polite urbanity and to the affable and slightly amused attitude of a man who's lived a full and exciting life and reserves judgment on it that I'm never quite sure whether he's more or less deceptive than he appears.

"I came up because Mrs. Whitney asked me to," I answered casually. "And of course Washington isn't the same when you're away."

He cocked his head down then and shot me an amused and quite unbelieving glance.

"And what are you doing up here?" I asked.

"I'm trailing some income-tax figures." He chuckled a little. "A rather well-known New Yorker. He had a fire, rather fortunately, and all his records were burned. Unfortunately, he didn't know all the banks he uses have had a microfilm recording system for the last fifteen years, so all his checks have had their pictures taken. That's what I was doing at the Quaker Trust. Odd you should have remembered Toplady's name. He's in charge of their records."

A bright and lovely light began to dawn in my mind. "Is it Myron's income tax, by any chance?" I asked. "Myron Kane's?"

He looked around at me again. "Good Lord, no! It's somebody you've met in Washington. He has no connection with Myron. Why?"

And I suppose I should add that he really hadn't, and that the job Colonel Primrose was on, furthermore, had nothing whatever to do with any of the Whitneys.

"I just wondered," I said. "When I said I was coming up, you seemed awfully interested in Myron."

"I am. Because of that profile of Whitney he's doing. The daughter and son-in-law are up in arms. I happened to see Ben Hibbs after they'd been in. Then I saw Myron. That was about a week ago. He certainly looked like Mark Twain's calmly confident Christian with four aces. I've been wondering."

"Do you know Judge Whitney well?" I asked.

We'd got to the Warwick Room. It was already crowded, as Philadelphians eat lunch earlier than any other people in the world.

He nodded. "And I'd hate to see Myron do one of his more malicious jobs on him. Most newspapermen have a sort of ethics, but Myron's haven't ever been visible to me."

It was a meatless day, but when the omelets came, they were very good.

"Myron's always seemed to me to have a chip on his shoulder, for some reason," Colonel Primrose said. "Inferiority complex is a more hackneyed way of saying it. I don't see why he has it. The Press Who's Who says he was born in Virginia and educated by tutors and in private schools abroad. Universities, London and the Sorbonne. His father was a judge and his mother a Randolph of Virginia. With that background, he oughtn't to be such a damned snob. He's made a lot of money and he knows the best people, and yet he delights in sideswiping everybody with any social standing. I wonder what he's doing to the Whitneys. Do you know?"

I shook my head and went on with my lunch. When I glanced up, he was looking at me with a politely amused smile on his face.

"You know what you remind me of?"

"No," I said. "And I'd just as soon not."

"Did you ever see a sooty grouse fluttering around, pretending to have a broken wing, when you get too near her covey?" he asked. "Myron hasn't been appealing to your better nature, has he? Or is it Mrs. Whitney?" He looked at me then in that oddly appraising way of his. "Who broke into Ben Hibbs' place last night, Mrs. Latham?" he asked deliberately.

I could feel my cheeks flush warmly. There's something very irritating about being an open book.

"I haven't the faintest idea," I said.

He paid his bill and got up. "I think you'd better come over to the *Post* with me. Unless you have some reason for not wanting to."

"Don't be silly," I said. "I'd love to."

That wasn't true, of course; I didn't want to go at all, and I wish now I hadn't.

It was the first time I'd ever been there. The taxi went skidding down Spruce Street. It was almost two o'clock. The gray brick between the car tracks was a shimmering gunmetal ribbon down the center of the old street, with its line of leafless sycamores on either side and its mellow, lovely old houses. We turned into Washington Square, across Walnut into 7th Street and to the right, weaving a perilous way through the enormous trucks unloading prodigious rolls of paper in the narrow alley of Sansom Street alongside the Curtis Building. Independence Square was just ahead of us, and the old State House, the cradle of liberty, where the bell is that rang out to all mankind, was on our left as we turned —so beautiful, and with so much dignity and meaning in its time-stained brick and slender, gleaming cupola, that I never see it without a sudden quickening of my heart. Men and women in uniform hurrying by gave it a sharpened meaning just then and as we turned right into 6th Street in front of the Curtis Building, the sun caught the great service flag hanging in front of the weather-stained double columns of the façade. The number "947" was on the single blue star in its radiant white red-bordered field.

We got out and went up the steps. It didn't at once seem strange to me that a policeman was standing behind the long plate-glass window at the left of the door or that Sgt. Phineas T. Buck's large, square and granite form was standing there with him. I've seen both Sergeant Buck and policemen in unexpected places everywhere. But Colonel Primrose, I thought, quickened his pace and pushed open the heavy bronze-trimmed door a little hastily. We stepped into the vestibule, and Colonel Primrose opened the plate-glass door at the left.

I knew, when we went in, that something was wrong, knew it the instant Sergeant Buck stepped forward, even before I saw the group of people there in the lobby. I'd seen groups of people look like that before, and heard the same sort of voice say, "Get back there, everybody. Get 'em back. Get 'em out of the way."

They were across the lobby in front of a raised terrace between square marble columns. Behind the terrace was the great glass mosaic, lustrous, softly glowing, the purple shadows creeping up among opalescent flowers around the brilliant waterfall at the base of a mountain to the glorious glow of the sunset and the dark mystery of gnarled and romantic trees. Then the soft musical trickle of water stopped abruptly. Someone was moving the ornamental shrubs around the front and side of the terrace. I saw a great terra-cotta oil jar, like Ali Baba's, being pushed away, and heard the voice again, "Get back. Get 'em back. . . . Here, doctor."

There was a movement in the tightly packed group. They parted to let a white-coated man through. I saw him then. He was lying, his face wet, at the side of a shallow, oblong pool. His black hair was clinging to his pallid face, and there were bits of green pond scum matted on it like grotesque vine leaves of the grave. It was Myron Kane, and he was quite dead.

"I guess he fainted and drowned," someone said.

I knew that wasn't so. Myron Kane had never for an instant fainted and drowned, not in the soft glow of the alabaster lights in front of the opalescent and green-and-gold mural—not anywhere. Myron's hold on life had been too ruthless and too canny to let it go so easily.

There was a sudden commotion at the side of the pool. A man thrust his hand into it and brought it up again.

"Don't look like he fainted to me," he said.

He was holding up a knife. It looked like a butcher knife from some kitchen of cutthroats, sharp-pointed as a poniard, razor-edged. The handle was wrapped in some faintly gleaming gunmetal-gray material.

A tall, stoop-shouldered man spoke.

"That's a cutting-down knife," he said. "From Electro-typing, on the ninth floor."

A quiet, fatherly-looking man in a dark gray suit walked over toward him. He could have been a member of the Rotary Club in good standing, a lawyer or an executive of The Curtis Publishing Company—anything except what I soon learned he was—the captain of the Philadelphia homicide squad.

Colonel Primrose went over, too, and spoke to him.

54

"I know this man," he said. He nodded toward the tall, stoop-shouldered man. "This is Erd Brandt. He was a colonel in the Seventh Regiment. He's one of the editors here."

"Yes?" the fatherly-looking man said. "He looks to me like a Number One suspect. How does an editor know what kind of a knife it is and where it comes from? I suppose Benjamin Franklin had it in his pocket."

Colonel Primrose looked at him. "Benjamin——"

"That's the story." He jerked a finger at a man sitting white-faced behind the marble desk at the side of the lobby near the elevator. "He's been sitting there since one o'clock. He says the last person he saw in here was Benjamin Franklin. My name's Francis X. Malone, and I'm captain of the homicide squad, and I'm Irish, and I've seen a lot of fairies, but Benjamin Franklin's dead. Maybe he founded this magazine, but he's still dead."

I had the grotesque thought that if it was Benjamin Franklin, it wasn't Monk, it wasn't anybody in Rittenhouse Square.

Captain Malone beckoned. The man at the desk got up and came over. He was white-faced and his knees were not steady, but he was in deadly earnest.

"I'm not kidding, captain," he said. "I saw him. I tell you I saw him with my own eyes. I mean, I know him. Look. I look at him all day." He pointed to the white marble bust of the great gazetteer looking placidly down from his pedestal. "He walked right across here. I saw him. He had on white stockings and a brown coat and short pants with buckles at the knees. I'm not crazy. I tell you I saw him twice."

A tall young man with blue eyes and glasses, quiet, calm and unhurried, had come over to the table in front of the pool terrace where we were.

"I tell you, Mr. Hibbs, I saw him—I saw Benjamin Franklin," the man from the desk said. And I had no possible doubt of the conviction of truth in his own mind. "I just tell you I saw him," he added patiently.

"All right, you saw him," Captain Malone said. "Just take it easy." He turned to Ben Hibbs. "Did all the members of your staff know this man Kane, Mr. Hibbs?"

Ben Hibbs nodded. "Yes. We all knew him."

"Did you like him?"

There was a little hesitation, not long, but a little too long. "Yes. Well enough." His blue eyes were slightly troubled as they moved over the group of men, some of them in shirt sleeves, some not, who had moved away from the terrace and the goldfish pool. He looked like a shepherd counting his flock.

Captain Malone watched him with a fatherly interest.

"Not all present, Mr. Hibbs?"

"No."

I looked quickly at Colonel Primrose. It seems incredible that I felt my heart glow a little. Not that I wanted anyone on *The Saturday Evening Post* to hang for the murder of Myron Kane, exactly. It was just that—— I was aware suddenly that the benevolent man in the dark gray suit was looking at me intently.

"I don't think you've met Captain Malone, have you, Mrs. Latham?" Colonel Primrose said.

I'd realized already that I'd made a mistake. But he couldn't connect the Whitneys with it, possibly. I hadn't said anything.

Just then somebody spoke up abruptly, "What's this?"

It was one of Captain Malone's detectives. They'd moved Myron Kane's body away from the pool. The man was holding up a small yellow oblong slip of paper.

And another man spoke. "That's a manuscript number. It's attached to the manuscript up in the composing room. How the hell did it get down here?" It was a tall young beanpole of a man speaking. He was so loosely jointed, it was surprising he stayed together. "I'd better phone up to Composition," he said. "That's off of Kane's profile of Judge Whitney. Where in hell's the manuscript?"

Where indeed, I thought. I tried to look as if I was as surprised as everybody else. But I knew before Bob Fuoss came back from the telephone that Myron's profile of Judge Whitney had disappeared.

"All I need now is for somebody to tell me Benjamin Franklin took it," Captain Malone said gently.

7

That numbered slip of yellow-colored paper that Captain Malone held in his hand looked very small and innocuous, but in effect it was a streak of chain lightning. In one flash it linked the murdered body of Myron Kane, lying there beside the goldfish pool in the marble lobby of The Curtis Publishing Company in Independence Square, in front of that glass mosaic of a sunset garden, with the manuscript of his profile of Judge Whitney and with the Whitneys themselves, due west in Rittenhouse Square. Or so it seemed to me, with the background of the last twenty-four hours that I had. It apparently wasn't that simple to the chief of the homicide squad. Captain Malone listened quietly when Bob Fuoss, the managing editor, came back from the telephone at the reception desk.

"I called Composition, on the ninth floor," he said. "That's off of the manuscript of Kane's piece on Judge Whitney. It was sent to the monotype keyboard this morning. The foreman—Alexy—says it was in his basket on his desk when he went out for lunch."

Captain Malone's eyes moved slowly toward the pool and to the knife with its razor edge and stiletto point that somebody had put on the refectory table in the center of the lobby. A little green scum from the bottom of the pool was clinging moistly to the gunmetal-colored adhesive tape wrapped around the handle. "Ninth floor," he said meditatively. He nodded at the knife. "And that came from the ninth floor too?" He was deliberate and quiet-spoken. "I guess somebody knew his way around. I went through the plant once, and I couldn't make heads or tails of it myself."

He seemed to be listening, and it wasn't till I noticed that that I became aware of the low rumble of the presses that throbbed and vibrated all around us, like the roar of far-distant but continuous thunder. You didn't notice it at first, and when you did, it was hard to tell whether you were hearing it with your ears or feeling it through the soles of your feet. I found out later, when I went over there, that the thick, fireproof wall behind the bronze doors of the elevators, extending from Walnut Street clear through the building to Sansom Street and dividing manufacturing from the editorial and business divisions, was what kept it from being completely deafening.

Captain Malone turned to Fuoss. "I'll start at that end, and I'll need somebody to show me around. You get your people back where they belong. I'll be around after a while."

Four men came through the plate-glass double doors—one of them with a camera, two with a stretcher. Captain Malone motioned the little group of *Post* editors and Colonel Primrose and me toward the elevators. We stood there avoiding one another's eyes as the four men set to work. They didn't know Myron Kane. He was nothing now; he could be pushed around and carted off as a part of the job they made their living at. It didn't seem that that ought to happen quite that way to Myron Kane, with his Homburg and his stick and his London-tailored overcoat, just as it happened to anybody who'd never seen a sultan or told an ambassador what a prime minister had said. All the arrogance and ego and ability that had made Myron a dramatic figure, whether one had any affection for him or not, were gone, and I think we were all a little ashamed that that was the way it was.

Malone's fatherly gaze rested on the editors. "Just give your names to the sergeant here," he said. "Go on about your business. I'll be in touch with you."

I had the idea there was a feeling of relief that I wasn't the only one to share. I saw one editorial Adam's apple that had been traveling like an agitated plumb bob over an open shirt collar and loosely knotted orange-and-black knit tie take a sudden nose dive and flutter back to normal. There was a deliberate and well-mannered exit into the elevator—I mean, no editor trampled on any other to get in—but it was done with extraordinary dispatch. They stood waiting for Ben Hibbs, who was talking to Colonel Primrose—a very sober and moist-browed group of men, uncomfortably aware of the relentlessly paternal eye of Captain Malone fixed on them. I could see them visibly relaxing as the bronze door closed at last, leaving Colonel Primrose and me still down there with the chief of the homicide squad and the man who had seen Benjamin Franklin.

I gave my name and Abigail Whitney's address to the sergeant. The man at the desk wiped his forehead with his handkerchief and looked at me.

"They think I'm crazy," he said hopelessly. "But I tell you I was sitting here sorting out the cards." He pointed at the stack of interview cards by the house phone on the desk. "A lot of people came in all at once, right after lunch. Then I was filing the duplicates we keep to check up on anybody still in the building. I just happened to look up, and there was Benjamin Franklin—funny clothes and all."

He pointed to the candelabrum with the carved pedestal next to the fluted pillar and the bust of Franklin.

"He was walking right across there. I thought it was funny, but you get used to all sorts of cockeyed gags around this place, and he looked like he knew where he was going, all right. He gets over in front of the table and stops and looks all around, and walks up on the terrace behind all those trees they got stuck around, and in a minute he comes out and walks on over there toward Personnel, and then he just disappears. I don't see him go or anything. I think to myself, *Gee, that's funny,* and first thing I know, I turn around, and here he is right by me. He's looking straight through the columns, and his arm's up, pointing over at the pool, I guess. I look over and I don't see anything. All I see is those two guys coming in the door."

He nodded toward the ink and paper salesmen talking to the detectives by the window.

"I look around again, thinking I must be going bats, and he's gone again. There's a girl coming down the stairs." He pointed to the narrow flight of steps going up at the side of the elevator shaft. "I say, 'Did you meet anybody going upstairs?' and she says, 'No,' and goes on across over there, just when those two fellows start over to look at the mosaic picture. She goes right on past them, and all of a sudden one of them lets out a yell, and that's the first I know anything happened to Mr. Kane."

As he talked, he kept shuffling the small stack of unfiled appointment cards. I could see the names on them, and I saw Myron's, but no other that I knew.

Captain Malone and Colonel Primrose came over.

"You keep a record of everybody who comes into the building?"

The man opened a drawer and took out a small file. "These are today's," he said. "Before one o'clock."

"I suppose there are other entrances," Captain Malone said.

"Just the two in Sansom Street. They keep a check there too. Nobody can get in without giving his name."

"Except the people in the building. How many? A couple thousand of 'em?"

"But they're all known," the man said. "Or if they aren't, they have to show their passes. We know everybody this side. Only first-register people come in here. That's executives, editors and their private secretaries. They use this elevator. There's another one for second-register people over there on the other side for office employees who come in at Sixth and Sansom. The men in the plant use the one at Seventh and Sansom."

"When did Kane come in?"

"Half past one."

The man picked out Myron's card and handed it to him.

"To see Mr. Fuoss," he said. "That's the tall, lean one."

"Did you see him come down?" Captain Malone asked.

"No, sir, I didn't. There was a crowd of Circulation people in around two, and he could have come down in the elevator while I was writing down their names. They were all here at the desk, and you have to call up and see if it's all right for each one of them to go up. They don't let anybody be in the place without knowing about it."

Captain Malone had been going through the cards in the morning file. As he put them down on the marble-top desk and reached for the afternoon stack, his coat sleeve knocked the pile a little crooked. The one on top was for somebody named Bergman. The one underneath was also staring me in the face. It was for Mr. Samuel Phelps, to see Mr. Fuoss. The appointment was for 12:05. *Mr. Samuel Phelps,* I thought. *Soapy Sam. Elsie Whitney's husband.*

"I don't see," Captain Malone said benevolently, "if the manuscript they're talking about was swiped between twelve and twelve-thirty, how anybody could hang around here until two o'clock to murder this fellow unless he belonged here. It looks to me——"

The house phone buzzed. The man picked it up, listened for an instant and handed it to Captain Malone.

He listened silently. "Okay, hold everything," he said. "I'll be up."

He turned back to Colonel Primrose. "It looks the same

60

way still," he said placidly. "The knife disappeared at lunch-time too. The fellow that owns it had to borrow one when he got back at twelve-thirty. I don't like to disagree with you, colonel, but, so far, it looks like an inside job to me. Anyway, the Whitneys are high-class people. But we'll go into that."

Sam Phelps' appointment card was still lying almost full-face at the top of the pile, but neither of them had so far connected it with the name of Whitney. It would happen sooner rather than later, I knew from long experience.

Captain Malone looked at me. "Colonel Primrose tells me you're staying at Judge Whitney's sister's house and that Kane was there, too, Mrs. Latham. If you'll stop around at the police station, Twelfth and Pine, tomorrow morning, let's say, if that's convenient, I won't keep you now."

He went on, taking with him the file with Sam Phelps' name in it, and I looked at Colonel Primrose. I was still too astonished and too upset to think of anything to say. I couldn't have been more taken aback.

"Don't be silly," he said curtly. "You're not in Washington, and Malone's not Captain Lamb. This couldn't be kept away from Rittenhouse Square, and there's no use trying. We're going up to the *Post* now."

"I," I said, "am going back to Rittenhouse Square."

"That's exactly where you're not going. You're coming with me."

The elevator door clanged shut behind us. "Sixth floor," Colonel Primrose said. We went up in a grim silence.

In the marble foyer on the sixth floor, another bust of Benjamin Franklin stood on another pedestal at the left. There was a narrow staircase at the right, the continuation of the one the receptionist thought Benjamin Franklin must have gone up, but that the girl coming down hadn't met him on. It extended up to an iron-railed raised platform across the end of the foyer. Under it, an iron grille was set in the wall. Men's voices were coming through it, their owners obviously unaware they could be heard outside, and reasona-bly, I suppose, as it turned out to be the men's washroom. And it was hard to believe that they were part of the same subdued and silent group that had been wilting under Cap-tain Malone's spurious benevolence downstairs less than ten minutes ago. They were all talking at once.

". . . been asking for it . . . first-rate heel."

"Where's Pete?"

"Pipe down about Pete."

"Did you see the royal brush-off he gave the colonel?"

"A primrose by a river's brim, a simple Primrose was to——"

"I don't get who'd want to murder the guy."

"Me."

"Me too. I hated his——"

"He burned me up."

"Who pinched the script?"

". . . who'd know the ropes?"

"Pete——"

"I said pipe down about Pete."

"Come on, you goons; the dicks'll be up here——"

". . . and shut up about the row."

"We'll all be in the clink if you don't pipe down."

Colonel Primrose had stopped and was listening, deliberately and intently, his face oddly uneasy. I didn't understand. It was quite obvious that none of the three men whose voices we could hear was seriously perturbed about himself or any of the immediate *Post* staff.

But that was before Captain Malone had had any of them over at 12th and Pine, of course, and before his men had found the graphite smudges on the washroom door, and before they found out where the man they called Pete had really been.

The *Post* editorial offices make a sort of hollow half rectangle along the 6th Street front of the building. Outside the editor's office is a dark wood rail barrier past a reception desk and a Gargantuan soft-cushioned sofa, and the swinging gate has a defective hinge. It hippity-hopped and limped shut behind Colonel Primrose and me. In Ben Hibbs' office, a desk stood in front of the windows, with an easy chair by it, complete with ottoman for the editorial legs to stretch out on. There seems to be something about reading manuscripts that makes it impossible for editors to keep their feet on the ground. At the moment, however, with a manuscript missing and the author of it dead, nobody was concerned with reading. The Editor, Bob Fuoss and Erd Brandt, the senior associate editor, were in a huddle at the end of a long table in the center of the Chinese rug. They stopped talking abruptly.

"We're going to try to figure this out," Ben Hibbs went on then. "That doesn't mean you birds are going to turn into amateur detectives. Colonel Primrose will handle that. And the fewer wisecracks anybody makes, the less trouble we're going to have with Captain Malone's gang. And no talking outside." He nodded to Colonel Primrose.

"Are all the members of the staff here?" Colonel Primrose asked.

"Here or accounted for," Bob Fuoss said. "Stu Rose is in the hospital with a gentleman rider's busted vertebra. It's Bob Murphy's day in New York getting fiction material. Warner Olivier's in Washington for the week. Fred Nelson and Marion Turner are extremely busy. They'll be available as soon as the daily double's in. Now, if Kane had been editor of the *Racing Form*——"

"Where's Pete?" Colonel Primrose inquired placidly.

There was a short silence.

"You mean Pete Martin?" someone asked, and someone else said, "He'll be here in a minute."

I thought there was a tinge of uneasiness in the air.

Colonel Primrose turned to Fuoss. "Kane was in to see you, I understand. What time?"

"He came in at half past one. He wanted his script on Judge Whitney to make some corrections. I told him he could wait and make 'em in proof, because it had gone to the composing room. I was beginning to get sore, because he'd already called my secretary this morning and been told the same thing. He was nervous as a cat. I asked him if he'd put anything in that would get us in trouble, and he said no, he just wanted to polish it a little more. I told him it was a hell of a time to think of that, but he could polish the proof. Then I told him I was busy, and to get out, and he said he was waiting for a phone call. I told him he could wait somewhere else."

Another man who had just come in spoke. "He waited in my office, next door. But that's all right. I'm used to it. Everybody waits there. I don't have to make my living."

This was Day Edgar, I learned, and he spoke with a solemn and plaintive note of long suffering. He also spoke with one of the voices we'd heard through the grille in the washroom.

"He got his phone call at ten minutes past two. I had one to make, and I had to go into Stuart Rose's office to make it. He was gone when I came back."

More editors had come in.

"I saw him go to the elevator—my door's directly in front

63

of it," one of them said. It was Jack Alexander, a quiet, plumpish young man who was contemplating the point of his pencil on the pad in front of him. "I didn't see him go down, because I went into Art Baum's office, so he wouldn't see me and come back and talk all afternoon. That was about a quarter past two. If Kane ever got in and started shooting the breeze, you couldn't get him out."

"He was alone at the elevator?"

"So far as I know, he was."

"This profile of Judge Whitney," Colonel Primrose said. "Have you got a copy here?"

Bob Fuoss shook his head. "We had only the one that was on the ninth floor."

There was a copy at my house in Georgetown or in the mail on its way there, I thought suddenly.

"How many of you read it?" Colonel Primrose asked.

Five of them had—the Editor, Bob Fuoss, Jack Alexander and Art Baum, all article men, and of course Harley Cook. None of the associate editors primarily concerned with fiction had read it.

"Was there anything explosive in it?"

All shook their heads.

"We wouldn't have taken it," Fuoss said. "So far as I could see, it was a straightforward and interesting piece. There were a few cracks at the family. They were amusing, and not so malicious as Kane's stuff usually was. I'd told him we weren't interested in taking the hide off anybody."

Colonel Primrose had started to speak, when Fuoss suddenly brought his chair down on its front legs.

"Phelps!" he exclaimed. "Mr. Samuel Phelps. Judge Whitney's son-in-law. He was here this noon. Who saw him?" He looked around the blank faces at the table. "They called up from the lobby and said he was there and wanted to see me, just before twelve. He never showed up. You don't think——"

He broke off abruptly, pushed back his chair and was out of the room in a couple of strides. In a second, he was back again.

"He never showed up at all," he said. "Miss Ganz waited for him till a quarter to one. She called the desk back, but they hadn't seen him."

"You're not saying," a skeptical voice said, "that Mr. Samuel Phelps whipped up to the ninth floor, pinched Myron's script and beat it without anyone seeing him, are you? Did you ever try to find your way around the ninth floor?"

The idea of the pompous and respectable Mr. Sam Phelps whipping around anywhere stealing manuscripts seemed pretty ludicrous to me.

"All I'm saying is he didn't show up in my office," Fuoss said. "I waited ten minutes and forgot about him. I had a date."

"Tell Captain Malone the date was at a poolroom on Market Street and you'll ruin the magazine."

That came from Art Baum, whose round face looked like that of a surprised if slightly weatherbeaten cherub.

"Brother in sin, it's the only alibi we've got."

The editor smiled a little dryly. "It will look fine in the magistrate's court. Two of the editors playing three-cushion billiards for a tuna-fish sandwich; two of them—including the first lady—going across town to place bets on the horses with a headwaiter. Didn't somebody take a world-famous author out to lunch?"

"The Fifth Freedom," someone said, "is the Freedom from Authors once a week."

"I don't think Captain Malone is going to be as much interested in what you were doing at noon," Colonel Primrose said, "as in what you were doing between a quarter past two and a quarter to three."

Someone interrupted abruptly. "Here he comes."

I heard the sound of heavy steps outside, and the limping hippity-hop of the gate swinging back into place. A very large man with very blue eyes and a flushed face, his shock of iron-gray hair parted in the middle, filled the door. He wiped a rather sheepish grin off his face and got himself into a seat, flushing a still brighter red.

"You know Pete Martin, Colonel Primrose," Ben Hibbs said.

Before Colonel Primrose could speak, Captain Malone and a thin-faced, worried-looking man I hadn't seen before came through the door, followed by two detectives.

"I'm through on the ninth floor, colonel," Malone said. "I'd be glad if you'll have a look around up there. Mr. Hamilton here will take you up. You couldn't find your way around."

Colonel Primrose hesitated for an instant and nodded, and we followed Mr. Hamilton out. He was from the manufacturing side of the Curtis company.

"There's no way across to Manufacturing on this floor," he said when we got to the elevator. "There's a fireproof wall divides the two sides, Editorial and Manufacturing. We'll go down to the fifth and over and up the other side."

The noise of the machinery was deafening over there—the roar of presses and cutting machines and binders. It was like being in an inferno of thunder and speed. The floors were sticky with paraffin, it was hot as sin, and the jets overhead that humidified the air and kept down static electricity from the great rolls of paper whirring through the rollers sounded like a million snakes hissing at once. We walked miles, it seemed to me, through more fireproof walls and huge metal doors. Myron Kane was dead, but one million two hundred thousand magazines had to be printed that day.

By the time we'd got into a freight elevator and gone up four floors, past the great double-X presses that roared even louder, to the electrotyping division, I felt as if I'd been through a perfect mechanized bedlam.

It wasn't quite so thunderous and Gargantuan on the ninth floor, but it looked even more complicated. We walked back another city block through it, and got to the foundry. A couple of detectives were there, and some of the Curtis people. Mr. Hamilton turned us over to Mr. Trayser, who was head of all the babel we'd come through.

We went over by the detectives. I saw a long bench covered with graphite, and on it wax impressions of each complete and final page of the magazine on heavy metal. There were also three knives on the bench like the one they'd fished out of the goldfish pool. A good-looking young man covered with graphite, except for his face, which was clean and shining as an apple, was shaving off the excess ridges of wax on the plates with still another knife, like a woman shaving off the extra pastry around the edge of a pie. His name was Andrew Hesington, and it was his knife that had disappeared.

He nodded to Colonel Primrose. "I left it right here when I went up to the tenth-floor cafeteria for lunch," he said. "Of course I recognize it. I've had it ten years. I had it made myself. It's one-hundred-ten-carbon steel and fits my wrist. I always leave it here, and it was here at twelve and wasn't here at twelve-thirty. That's all I know. I never heard of Myron Kane."

Mr. Trayser took us on through another open fire door to the composing room. It was a little more comprehensible to

66

me here. The proofreaders were on one side, and a group of women were sitting at machines with typed manuscripts on racks beside them, copying them on the monotype keyboard. And directly on the main aisle of the huge room was the foreman's desk.

"That manuscript was right here," Mr. Trayser said. He pointed to a basket at the side of the desk. "It comes over from *Post* Editorial and stays here till we get to it. If it hadn't been for that Composition slip, nobody would have noticed it was gone; it could have been gone until somebody from *Post* Editorial called up and asked for it." He shook his head. "This has never happened before.

"I don't know who would know where to come to get a manuscript," Mr. Trayser continued. "I can't believe that any of our employees——" He shook his head again.

"You have a good many new ones, probably," Colonel Primrose said.

"Yes. Filling in for those in the service."

"Then if a man took off his coat and rolled up his sleeves and walked in here as if he knew what he was doing, it's ten to one nobody would have stopped him?"

"That's true, colonel. But he'd have to know his way about. You see, it isn't easy."

Colonel Primrose nodded. "He would also have to know where the manuscript was at that exact time," he said slowly. "Which would be harder still, for an outsider." He stood there for a moment, looking down at the desk and the basket, and over at the keyboard. "The foreman?" he said then.

Mr. Trayser nodded. The keyboard foreman came up. His face had a look of mingled surprise and indignation, and the surprise increased at Colonel Primrose's question.

"I was wondering," Colonel Primrose said quietly, "if you had a call about this manuscript this morning?"

The foreman stared. "I was going to tell somebody about it," he said. "Somebody called up from *Post* Editorial and asked where it was. I told them it had gone to the keyboard. Now they tell me they didn't call."

Colonel Primrose's black eyes sparkled. "Did he give his name?"

"Oh, sure. I wouldn't give anybody any information unless I knew who I was talking to—or thought I did. I recognize some of the voices, like Mr. Fuoss'. I don't like to say, now he says it wasn't him. But he said it was W. Thornton Martin."

"That's Pete Martin?" Colonel Primrose asked.

Mr. Trayser and the foreman nodded.

"I thought it was funny he didn't just say 'Pete Martin' instead of 'W. Thornton,' " the foreman said. "But he used to be art editor before, and that's not my department, so I don't know his voice. But that's who he said it was. And nobody in here took that manuscript, Mr. Trayser. I know all these people. They wouldn't do anything like that."

"Thank you," Colonel Primrose said politely.

We went on. The composing room seemed to be practically the whole side of the building. At the end of it, we were back to the fireproof wall dividing Manufacturing from Editorial. There was an open fire tower with a broad staircase at either end, but no one had gone out that way. There was also an elaborate series of service elevators, air shafts and ventilators, closets and storeroom and washrooms, a telephone pay booth and a tunnel leading across to the women employees' cafeteria on the ninth floor of the publication side.

We got to the front elevator again.

In the lobby, Captain Malone's men were gone, except for one detective standing by the door. Myron Kane was gone. So was the man who had seen Benjamin Franklin. One of the watchmen had taken his place at the desk. The colors in the great glass mosaic had changed and deepened, as if the sun had really set behind the purple shadows of the gnarled, fantastic trees. There was a sense of emptiness in the marble hall, and a silence so profound that the vibration of the great presses on the other side of the wall hummed audibly.

"Will you tell Mr. Hibbs I'll see him later?" Colonel Primrose said to Mr. Trayser, who'd stopped at the door with us.

He started to push it open, and stopped. He was looking at my hands. I looked at them too. My gloves, that had been clean when I came, were absolutely gray with the graphite dust from the bench where the cutting-down knife had come from. It was a little startling, because I had no memory of touching anything there.

The colonel looked at his own hands. They were grimier than my gloves. Then he glanced at the plate-glass door in front of us. The detective standing there looked at it too. The whole side of the thick glass was covered with blurred fingerprints where people had gone out all day.

"Did Captain Malone have this fingerprinted?" Colonel Primrose asked.

The detective shook his head. "Waste of time. What would you get but a lot of blobs?"

Mr. Trayser went outside with us.

"It may be a waste of time," Colonel Primrose said, "but I'd be glad if you'd have those doors propped open and left for me. Graphite has a way of sticking. The handle of that knife was covered with it. And it's like blood—there are spots where you don't think of looking."

If it didn't come so close to that had-I-but-known sort of thing that's so irritating, I would say that at that moment Colonel Primrose had the gift of the prophetic tongue.

8

There was no question, of course, of "had I but known" about why I'd been taken on the educational tour of the ninth floor of the Curtis Building. Nor why Colonel Primrose hadn't stopped on the sixth floor on the way down, instead of sending a message by Mr. Trayser. He wanted to see the Whitneys before anyone else did.

And it was his anxiety not to waste time about it, I suppose, that made him start down the steps without seeing the little man across the street. He was not easy to see. He was as drab and colorless as the barren earth of Independence Square behind him. Conscious as I'd become of his existence in the last twenty-four hours, I wouldn't have noticed him if it hadn't been for the policeman who was keeping the street clear. He had stopped and was looking over our side, and the policeman took two or three steps across the car tracks. "Move on, there. I've told you twice now. Move on."

That was when I saw it was Albert Toplady, and by then he was moving on. He was going quickly, but I thought unsteadily, and it occurred to me that he must have known what had happened.

The policeman came back. "You wonder what they expect to see," he said. "That guy's been hanging around the last hour or more."

"It might be a good idea to find out why," Colonel Primrose said placidly.

We went along, leaving the policeman looking a little startled. I glanced at Colonel Primrose. I couldn't tell whether he'd recognized Mr. Toplady or not. It didn't occur to me, until we got to the corner, that having none of the background I had on Mr. Toplady and his letter which he had given me to deliver to Myron Kane, and the mess that somebody taking it from Abigail Whitney's room had

70

caused, he had no reason to be concerned over the little man's presence there, even if he'd recognized him as the bookkeeper who hadn't showed at the bank that morning. He hadn't seen Myron Kane turn a sick gray-green at the mention of Albert Toplady's name or heard him at the foot of the stairs outside Abigail Whitney's room, broken-voiced and shaken, saying he'd be ruined if the letter wasn't found. Nor had he heard Judge Whitney at Travis Elliot's house, talking about irreparable harm.

Perhaps, I thought, the policeman should have stopped him, and at that point I think I would have said something myself, if I'd had a chance. But there weren't any cabs in sight and there was a streetcar on the corner. A lot of other people were getting into it, and by the time we'd got to the door, Mr. Toplady had disappeared, going along the square as fast as he could in the direction of the water front.

It seemed ridiculous anyway. Unless Albert Toplady was a consummate actor, which seemed unlikely, I could have sworn he had no wish or intention to ruin Myron Kane by writing him a letter. The breathless awe with which he'd spoken of his being at Mrs. Whitney's, the way he'd called him the great foreign correspondent, were too earnestly sincere to mask any attempt to injure him. And at that point I got such an abrupt shock that Mr. Toplady went completely out of my mind.

We'd got into the crowded streetcar. When I got my balance back from the jack-rabbit start it made across 6th Street, I found myself facing right, looking down at the front of the Curtis Building. Coming down the steps was Sgt. Phineas T. Buck, and with him was a girl. That in itself was extraordinary enough, but the startling thing was that the girl was Laurel Frazier. I could have mistaken the gray Persian-lamb coat with the black velvet collar, but there was no mistaking the crown of auburn curls above it.

In the brief glimpse I got as the car crossed the street, she was holding out her hand to him. I didn't see any more, but that was enough. The fact that she was coming out of the building meant she had been in it, and it just wasn't the place for Judge Whitney's secretary to be at that time. Not, I thought, if anybody else had overheard the scene between her and Myron Kane in the Broad Street Station the afternoon before—or even if they hadn't.

I looked at Colonel Primrose, disturbed about him, too, as a matter of fact. He was apparently too involved in his own

71

thoughts to have noticed. He had never been so silent and uncommunicative in all the time I'd known him, and I didn't like the set of his jaw or the obsidian chill in his eyes as they met mine over the orange-feathered hat of the colored woman between us in the aisle. I was even a little frightened. There's a sign up in the Curtis Building, which I saw later, that might have saved me a lot of trouble if I'd seen it then and taken it to heart. It says, "Each and every member of this staff MUST CONSTANTLY bear in mind that conduct savoring of bullheaded obstinacy or any lack of proper consideration and politeness in dealing with each other in the conduct of this business is strictly prohibited." But, like most people, I probably wouldn't have realized it was I who was being bullheaded and obstinate anyway. Having been told so many times—and by Colonel Primrose himself—to keep out of other people's affairs, I no doubt would have convinced myself that that was what I was at long last doing.

We got off the streetcar at the corner of Rittenhouse Square and went along to Abigail Whitney's.

Colonel Primrose turned to me. "Tell Mrs. Whitney, when you see her, that I'd like very much to talk to her," he said equably. "I'll be at her brother's next door until I hear from her. Please tell her also that I'd like to see Myron's room." He turned at the door. "If you can make Mrs. Whitney understand that Myron's being a guest in her house imposes some pretty definite obligations, it would be wise to do so. Good-by."

I watched the door close behind him, not entirely sure that he wasn't saying a good deal more than was immediately apparent. He was as urbane as usual, but rather grimly so. I wondered if he thought the Whitneys were involved in either the disappearance of the manuscript or Myron's death, whether he could hope there'd be much in the way of tangible evidence left up there by now.

I started up the stairs. At the first mirror, I was aware that if Abigail Whitney was resting, she was doing it by her own unique method of Concentrating on Something Else. And as I rounded the head of the stairs, I could see Elsie Phelps even plainer. She was standing in the door, as irritatingly smug as before, and quite in control of the situation whatever it was or was to be.

"Oh, Mrs. Latham," she said, "my aunt would like to see you. We're dreadfully sorry about all the trouble we've put you to."

I didn't know whether she was being callously efficient or just didn't know. She gave me the kind of smile the lady of the manor might give to a feeble-minded member of the village canning society, and stepped back for me to go in.

Abigail Whitney was sitting up against her yellow cushions, bright-eyed and erect, alert and chipper as a sparrow. Standing in front of the carved-marble mantelpiece was Elsie's husband, Sam Phelps, the light glancing off his polished bald head. He was looking very imposing and immaculate indeed, and if there was a smudge of graphite on him, it was certainly not visible. His ego was blooming like a cabbage rose and, in fact, there was an air of complacent triumph about both of the Phelpses that was a little hard for me to take, with the image of Myron Kane's pallid face, the weeds from the pool dripping from his black hair, still haunting my memory.

"Oh, Dear Child," Abigail Whitney said. She held out her hand to me. "You must forgive me for not seeing your detective. But Sam has Settled Everything."

I looked at him, my mouth open, I suppose. He tilted back on his heels, his gold watch chain inscribing a slightly pompous arc across his piqué-piped vest, and nodded his head. As irony it was superb, but I couldn't tell. At least it seemed impossible that Elsie knew Myron was dead. She looked too pleased and proud. And Abigail Whitney was looking at Sam Phelps as I imagine she'd looked at men all her life—that sort of "isn't he wonderful?" look that no man born of woman seems immune to at any age.

"We should have left it in this Dear Boy's hands from the beginning." Her voice was soft as rose-colored velvet. "He's got Myron's letter back for him. We're going to get the document Laurel gave him. And there's nothing in the Profile of my Brother anyone can seriously object to. Sam has read it. I know you will be very pleased, Dear Child. Now we can All Relax." She started to, and stopped. "We should let All the Rest of them know," she said brightly.

I thought Sam looked a little troubled. "There's just one thing, Aunt Abby. I wouldn't want the judge to know I edited the manuscript in any way. I don't quite know how he'd like it."

"I do, Dear Boy," Mrs. Whitney said promptly. "He'd be livid. I won't tell a soul. I wouldn't think of it. Grace here is a Friend."

Elsie and Sam Phelps looked at her and then at me, a little dubiously, I thought—as well they might.

Sam's laugh was slightly hollow. "You know the saying, Aunt Abby—if you would keep your secret from an enemy, tell it not to a friend. I don't mean the judge is an enemy, of course," he added hastily. "It's just that I prefer none of them to know I've seen the manuscript."

It was startling to hear Sam quoting from *Poor Richard's Almanack* so soon after the author's ghost had been seen stalking the marble lobby of the magazine he founded. However, as Sergeant Buck had quoted him about lying down with dogs, it might just be something in the home-town atmosphere.

Sam looked at his watch.

"How did you ever persuade them to let you see the script?" I asked.

I'm afraid my voice was a little too brightly casual. His watch stopped in the process of being returned on its gold leash to his vest pocket.

"You're not doubting my husband's word, are you, Mrs. Latham?"

I'm afraid Elsie was rather brighter than she looked.

"Not at all," I said hastily. "I was just curious."

"Well, we can't let the ladies be curious, can we?" Sam said. He spoke with magnanimous humor from a male Olympus. He put his watch the rest of the way into his pocket. "For your satisfaction, then, Mrs. Latham, Mr. Kane showed it to me. He explained he did not want to offend the family in any way."

There were several other questions I'd have liked to ask him—such as when and where and why Myron showed it to him, and why him instead of Monk Whitney—but I didn't dare.

He turned to Mrs. Whitney. "We'll stop by and speak to the judge. Thank you for lunch, Aunt Abby."

She looked at him blankly. "Of course, Dear Boy," she said then. "You did lunch with me, didn't you? I'm so forgetful. It's Old Age. Good-by."

At the door, Elsie Phelps turned. "You're sure the—the document that Laurel gave him is all right, Aunt Abby? That we are going to get it back, I mean? We must be sure, you know."

Abigail Whitney's blue eyes snapped fire. "Good-by, Elsie," she said curtly. "You may leave the door open."

She leaned back in her yellow cushions until they'd gone. Then she turned to me.

"You look very peaked, Dear Child," she said. "No doubt it's the water. Philadelphia water disagrees with many people."

Our eyes met across the table beside the curved mahogany swan's neck that formed the arm of her day bed. Her eyes were clear and vivid-blue, and alarmingly intelligent just then, looking very calmly into mine.

"You know Myron Kane is dead, don't you?" I asked.

For a moment I thought she was going to deny it, but she didn't.

"It was on the radio at four o'clock," she said quietly. "It said he had been murdered. It's . . . most unfortunate."

"Did it say the manuscript copy of the judge's profile was missing too?"

She looked at me a little longer over that. "No. They didn't say that."

"Did Sam know—about Myron, I mean?"

"Not that I am aware of," Abigail Whitney said. "They didn't bring the matter up, and I hardly considered it my business to inquire."

It was so calm and so cold-blooded, somehow, the way she said it, that I felt the only tears I shed for Myron Kane—and I think almost the only tears that were shed for him—spring up, burning the edges of my eyelids.

"Don't be sentimental, Grace," she said sharply. " 'An eye for an eye' isn't from *Poor Richard*, but it's an older moral law."

"How can you say that?" I cried. "Myron hadn't killed anybody. He hadn't even hurt anybody. If there was nothing in the manuscript and you're getting the judge's document back——" I stopped, staring at her.

Her blue eyes were fastened on mine. There was a smile behind them so faint that it was almost imperceptible. I thought I had recognized irony before, but there was no doubting it now. It was double-edged this time, with a little pity and rather more than a little scorn at what I realized was plain, unadulterated stupidity on my part. It had all been a kind of ghastly double-talk, every word she'd said, and even while I'd questioned it I'd let myself be taken in by it.

The horror I felt must have sounded in my voice. "You don't—you can't mean——"

Her voice couldn't have been calmer, and she'd gone back

75

to her emphasized speech. "I didn't mean anything, Dear Child," she said. "I'm very deeply shocked, and of course I'm more than happy to Co-operate with the Authorities in any way I can, limited as I am by These Four Walls. You may go over to my Brother's and tell your Policeman that if he wishes to see Myron Kane's room, you are at complete liberty to show it to him. . . . Will you close the door as you go out?"

I started out, probably rather unsteadily.

"Of course you realize," she said calmly, "that Laurel can now marry Travis without anxiety. You were disturbed about that last night. Surely you don't expect the World with a barbed-wire fence around it, do you, Dear Child?"

I didn't answer her. I just went out and closed the door, a little sick at my stomach. All I wanted to do was get out of the house, out of the orbit of that imperturbable and ruthless old fraud reclining on her yellow cushions, pretending to be bedridden—a puppet mistress, pulling the strings, ordering people's lives without moving a step. Ordering their lives and even their deaths, for there was no possible doubt in my mind that she was responsible for Myron's death, morally, if not actually and physically.

I went downstairs. At least I could go next door and tell Colonel Primrose he had permission to see Myron's room. He was doing it on his time, and if he wanted to waste it, it was his privilege. Abigail Whitney, I thought, was probably on her way up there at that very moment, taking a last look to see that nothing remained that would do him or the police, when they came, the slightest bit of good.

I opened the front door. It was not quite dark outside, but the shadows were closing in and the lights were already on in the square. I stepped out and started a little. The old squirrel was there, twitching his moth-eaten tail, looking back down the steps. He flashed around, and then fled when he saw I was not his friend, the butler. It seems silly to get information from a squirrel, but that's the way it was. As he came from the square only when someone came up on the stoop, it was evident that someone had been there. The way he was sitting, twitching his tail, looking down the steps, showed clearly that there had been an annoying hitch in the usual orderly procedure—visitor, butler, walnut—that he was accustomed to.

I looked quickly around the square. Retreating diagonally across 19th Street to the square was a small man in a gray

overcoat, and I recognized him this time. Mr. Albert Toplady was going rapidly, but not steadily.

I don't know whether I had a sudden change of feeling
about Mr. Toplady or whether it had been a cumulative
process. Up to that point and in spite of everything, I'd held
firmly to the idea that he was nothing really but a harmless
eccentric. I couldn't think so any longer. His being there on
Abigail Whitney's doorstep without ringing the bell and his
dashing off across the square were out of the bounds of
eccentricity. Added to what I could see now was actually a
pretty persistent haunting job he'd been doing on Myron
Kane, alive at the Broad Street Station and dead at the Curtis
Building, they seemed definitely sinister.

Mr. Toplady, I thought, must be either actively involved
in what was going on or he was a rather extraordinary bird
of evil omen, slightly molted, but appallingly accurate. And
the latter view was certainly devastatingly supported, and in
less than fifteen minutes flat. For if Laurel Frazier had set out
deliberately and with malice aforethought to tie a noose
around Monk Whitney's neck, she couldn't have done a more
workmanlike job on it.

I went over to Judge Whitney's brownstone house next
door and pressed the bell. A stiffly starched maid opened the
door, well past middle age, gray-haired and bony, but not
quite so heavily Irish as her counterpart at Abigail's. I explained that Colonel Primrose was there and that I had a
message to him from next door.

"If you'll come in, miss," she said. "The gentlemen are
busy just now, but Miss Frazier's here, and you can wait till
they're done."

Laurel Frazier was in the front room to the left. She could
well have been entitled Picture of a Young Lady Quietly
Going Out of Her Mind. She still had on her gray fur coat.
The wisp of gray felt that she used for a hat had been tossed,
with her bag and gloves, onto a long table against the wall,
and had fallen with one glove on the floor. The Irishwoman
picked them up.

"These gloves are a sight, miss," she said. She picked up the
other one. "How do you get so dirty? I'll just wash them out
for you."

I saw they were black—the fingers of them—the way mine
had been when I came off the ninth floor of the Curtis
Building.

She didn't seem to notice they were being taken away. She

77

was very distrait, her hair pushed back from her forehead, her eyes too bright and her face too pale. She had her hands in her coat pockets and looked as if she had been pacing up and down the rug in front of the coal fire burning in the grate. She stood there now in the middle of the room, waiting for the maid to go. When the door closed, she turned quickly to me.

"Where's Monk?" she asked sharply. "Have you seen him? I've got to get hold of him! I've simply got to!"

I shook my head. "I haven't seen him. Not since last night."

She made a quick gesture of despair and hopelessness. I don't know how to describe it, but it was terribly eloquent.

"I can't even find Travis," she said slowly. "His secretary said he'd heard about it—about Myron—and had left the office. I thought he'd come here. He must know we'll need him. I don't know what to do!" She started pacing again.

"Well, if you'll sit down and be quiet, maybe you can think of something," I said practically. "And what's the matter?"

Her eyes flashed wide open as she turned toward me and came back, "What's the matter? Don't you know?"

"I know Myron's dead," I said. "I don't know Monk needs a lawyer, if that's what you mean by trying to get hold of Travis. You certainly don't think Monk killed him."

Her face was dead and blank suddenly. She stood there silently a moment. When she spoke, her "No, of course not" lacked—and very noticeably lacked—any tone of ringing conviction.

"I wish I'd never seen Myron Kane," she said softly, after a minute. "It's all my fault. If it hadn't been for me——"

"Don't be silly," I said sharply. "You're jumping to a conclusion that may be just frantic. A lot of people didn't like Myron Kane."

She started to speak, and then glanced around sharply. A car had stopped in front of the house. The car door slammed, there was a sound of heavy feet on the concrete. Her face was white as she ran across to the front window and moved the velvet curtain aside just enough to see out. She flashed around.

"It's the police. They're coming in." She came quickly back, her eyes wide, looking at me with terror. "I've got to get rid of it," she whispered desperately. "They'll search the house; he told me they'd——"

I could hear the ring of the doorbell from the back of the house. The Irishwoman came plodding along the hall. Laurel Frazier took one look at the fireplace. The next instant she was over in front of it. She thrust her hand into her coat pocket and pulled something out. It was a tightly wadded ball of white cloth.

"Oh, don't!" I gasped.

It was too late. The white ball was in the fire and the flames spreading up over it. She grabbed the poker from the holder beside the hearth and jabbed it down under the coals. My heart sank.

The maid stopped by the door, sniffing.

"I smell something burning," she said. "Have you dropped a cigarette on the carpet?"

If Laurel had been white-faced before, she was whiter now. The smell of burning cloth was unmistakable.

"It's all right, Annie," she said breathlessly. "Go on to the door."

The instant the maid was out of sight, she did the most incredible thing. I caught my breath as she snatched up the corner of her coat, knelt down and thrust it into the fire. I expected to see the whole thing go up in a sheet of flame.

A voice as soft as a cat's tail came from the front door. "Is Judge Whitney in? Captain Malone, tell him. I'd like to——" The voice was still soft, but it spoke a little more quickly. "I smell something burning. What is it?"

"It must be my iron, sir," the maid said. "If you'll come in, please. The judge's secretary is here."

Laurel stood up quickly, the corner of her coat skirt burned black. She'd smothered the fire with her bare hands. She thrust them into her coat pockets and moved across the room to the door, her head erect. I'd never seen greater self-possession.

"I'm Laurel Frazier, Judge Whitney's secretary, Captain Malone," she said. "Will you come in?"

"Something is burning," Captain Malone said quietly. "It's in this room?"

"Yes, my coat," Laurel said. "I got too near the fire. It's my only coat too," she added ruefully.

The room smelled like a fire at a rummage sale. Captain Malone stood in the doorway, sniffing the air. Or he was there for an instant. I couldn't have believed anybody's mind —and body in this case—could move so fast. Before I was aware at all of what he was thinking, even, he was across the

79

room, the poker in his hand, delving through the flames into the coals in the bottom of the iron basket grate. Out came the blackened, evil-smelling wad. As the air struck it again, it burst into a pale pompon of flame on the green glazed tiles of the hearth. Captain Malone was down on his knees, smothering the flame with his brown pigskin glove, gently, as if the cloth were alive and could be hurt. Laurel Frazier stood motionless, white-faced again, her lips parted, staring at him.

9

Captain Malone got to his feet and looked around at her. "You shouldn't have done a thing like that, Miss Frazier," he said reproachfully. His voice was gentle as the morning dew, and his face was very grave and paternal as he shook his head at her—and the senior Hamlet's ghost never looked so much more in sorrow than in anger.

"Don't you see what you've done? Now I've got to begin thinking all over again. I've got to ask myself why Judge Whitney's secretary is so anxious for me not to know she's burning a piece of cloth that she spoils a coat to do it— because anybody can tell the difference. Cloth and fur don't smell the same when they burn. It's easy to tell when they've both been burned. You ought to have known that, oughtn't you?"

He was speaking as if to a three-year-old child, and she nodded her head not unlike one. He turned back to the hearth and knelt down, scooping up the black blob into an envelope he took out of his pocket. He went over to the table and put it down on a newspaper under the lamp, prying the burned layers off gently with the point of his silver pencil.

"When you want to burn anything," he said soberly, "don't wad it up. Just lay it out on top of the fire, where the air will get at it. You see?"

He looked over his shoulder at the girl staring stricken-eyed at the unfolding mass. The inside of the wadded cloth was untouched. It was still white—or it was except for the brown stains on it, and some of them not all brown yet, but still faintly red—red enough to show that blood could have made them. Captain Malone pulled very gently with his thumb and forefinger. I saw it was a handkerchief, man's size, and in the corner he was pulling out there was an embroi-

81

dered monogram. He took out his spectacles and put them on.

"Let's see now," he said. "Here's an *M*. And here's *W*. And this is a *T*? Isn't that a *T*?"

Laurel said nothing.

"That wouldn't be the judge, for instance," Captain Malone said. "His name's Nathaniel."

He took two steps toward her. She was standing there with her hands still thrust deep down into her pockets. He put his own hands out, palms up, without saying anything, and waited. After a moment, she took hers out of her pockets and held them out. The palms were blistered, but not so badly as I'd been afraid they were going to be. He shook his head.

"Don't you see I've got to tell myself a young lady would have to think an awful lot of anybody to burn her coat and burn her hands like this to keep me from finding a handkerchief with somebody's blood on it?"

Her face flushed suddenly to the color of her hair. "That isn't so," she said quickly. "It's just something I—I found, and I thought—I thought it could be misinterpreted——"

She stopped short. I heard a key grating in the lock and the front door opening. Laurel's face turned white, then flushed deeply. She snatched her hands out of Captain Malone's and thrust them back into her pockets. Something alive and alert moved in Captain Malone's eyes as he looked from her face to the door.

Monk Whitney was in the hall in the process of putting his battered gray felt hat on the table. He looked around, a very sober-faced young man even before he saw any of us. He came across the hall then, looking from one of us to the other.

"Smells like the city dump in here," he said. "What goes on?" He looked at Captain Malone. "My name's Whitney. You're the chief of homicide, aren't you?"

Captain Malone nodded. "Would your middle initial be *T*, by any chance?" he asked gently.

"A guessing game?" Monk inquired. His glance from one to the other of us was sardonic. "I'll bite, anyway. My middle initial is *T*. For Tyler. Monckton Tyler Whitney. What's the catch?"

Captain Malone motioned toward the unsavory mess lying on the morning paper. "This yours?"

Monk looked at it for an instant. "Not to recognize. Why?"

"It's got your initials on it," Captain Malone said. "And quite a lot of blood. Or I'd guess it's blood; I wouldn't want to say for sure till it's analyzed. The young lady hasn't told me yet where she found it or why she was trying to burn it up."

I thought that when Monk looked at Laurel Frazier, the chief of homicide must have been puzzled. It would have been hard to imagine anything more impersonal and detached than his level gaze.

"Does the young lady say it belongs to me, whatever it is?" he inquired politely.

"The young lady hasn't said anything," Laurel said hotly. "And she doesn't intend to say any more."

The sudden shower of blue sparks flying around must have been a further blow to what I suppose Captain Malone's theory was. He looked from one to the other of them and returned to the handkerchief. It was a rather elaborate arrangement, with interlacing letters embroidered in tan on the white linen inside a medallion.

Monk glanced at it. "I suppose it's mine if it's got my initials on it," he said casually. "Maybe I got it for Christmas. I don't pay much attention to such items, plain or fancy."

"Perhaps the one you've got with you is like this," Captain Malone said gently.

Monk started to put his hand in his pocket and stopped. "As a matter of fact," he said calmly, "I just remember. I don't happen to have one. My valet neglected to lay it out this morning."

Captain Malone's eyes brightened a little. "Maybe you'd just better tell me where you were today—say between twelve o'clock and three—if you don't mind."

"I'd be glad to, captain, but it just happens I can't."

"Why not, son?"

"Because where I was is my business. I don't mean to be offensive, captain. It's just a plain statement of fact. I wasn't at any time at The Curtis Publishing Company, if that's what you're getting at."

"I'm mighty glad to hear you say so," Captain Malone said benevolently. "Somebody was down there, and he's going to burn for it. I don't like murderers, and I don't care whether they live south or north of Market Street, Main Line or water front. I suppose you know Kane was murdered this afternoon?"

"Yes, I know it. I heard it on the radio."

Captain Malone looked at him steadily. He turned back to the table and began making a neat bundle of the burned handkerchief in the two top sheets of the newspaper.

"It seems to me the judge told me you were in the Army, son. Not out already, are you?"

"Marine Corps," Monk said shortly. "I'm on leave. I go back next week."

Captain Malone took a piece of string out of his pocket and tied it around his bundle. "You're out of uniform?"

"Exercise," Monk said calmly.

"You've been out exercising," Captain Malone said. "Not golf—you wouldn't hear a radio on a golf course, now, would you?"

Monk said nothing.

"And you wouldn't have been out walking. Your shoes would be wet if you had."

"I told you I wasn't going to tell you where I was today, Captain Malone," Monk said quietly. "And I meant it."

Captain Malone looked from him to Laurel, standing by the fireplace, her face expressionless. "You're making a mistake, both of you," he said earnestly. "I hope you'll think it over and come and see me." He put his little package carefully in his pocket. "Will you tell the judge I'm here?"

Laurel turned. "Colonel Primrose is in the library with him," she said. "Do you want to wait or——"

"I'll go up now, if it's all right with the judge," Captain Malone said. "The colonel's business and mine are pretty much the same, I guess."

Monk Whitney moved out of their way, deliberately avoiding looking at the girl.

"Will you tell Colonel Primrose, Laurel," I said, "that Mrs. Whitney says he's welcome any time he wants to go over?"

Captain Malone glanced at me sharply. It probably wasn't the most tactful way of delivering a message, but I didn't see any other way to do it. We heard their feet going up the stairs, and Monk turned promptly as they got to the top and started along the hall.

"Come on," he said. "Let's shove out of the fire trap and go get a drink. I could use a couple. Just wait till I get hold of that redheaded——"

84

"She was trying to get rid of that handkerchief," I interrupted. I was startled at the sudden resentment in his voice. "She really was."

"I'll bet."

He laughed or at least he made a sardonic noise. It could only be called mirthless. He picked up his raincoat.

"Come on, let's get out. Unless you don't want to be seen with——"

"Don't be funny," I said.

We went out and down the steps. Captain Malone's car, with a couple of detectives hunched up in the front seat, was parked on the other side of the street. There was a green coupé in front of the pink house next door. Monk took my elbow.

"Come on, quick," he said. "That's Trav's. He must be up with Abigail. I don't want to see him."

"Why not?" I was surprised at the sudden intensity in his voice.

"Why not? Good God, I should think you'd know."

We cut across in front of the police car to the square. He glanced back.

"It's not fair," he said. "They're not even watching us."

The reason was pretty obvious, I thought. Until Captain Malone caught Laurel red-handed, he'd refused to believe the Whitney clan could have had anything to do with Myron Kane's murder.

My bird of evil omen had flitted back. Mr. Toplady was sitting on a bench in the periphery of one of the hooded lights, gazing fixedly up at the second-story windows of the pink house across the street.

"Stop a minute," I said. "I want to speak to that man. Or go on. I'll catch up with you."

I stopped at the bench.

"Mr. Toplady," I said.

He started at the sound of his name, and looked around at me. I was appalled at his face. It was ashy-gray and haggard as an old dishrag. He stared at me dumbly, without any sign of recognition.

"I'm the woman you gave the letter to for Mr. Kane," I said. And I stopped. I didn't know quite how to go on.

He shook his head vaguely without speaking, just looking at me with a kind of helpless agony in his eyes. The light made the whites of them glitter a little, and I edged back a step, wishing I hadn't sent Monk on. He wasn't far, at that, just along to where the path intersected the circle, standing by a trash can, lighting a cigarette.

Mr. Toplady was still looking up at me.

"Don't you remember?" I asked.

"It doesn't matter," he said slowly. His voice was cracked and torn as if it hurt him to use it. "He's . . . dead now."

"I know. I'm terribly sorry."

He looked back at me, moving his head painfully.

I would have gone then, but as I moved to go something compelling in the haggard misery in his face held me there.

"Yes, he's dead," he mumbled. "They—they killed him. I know why." The words began to come faster, all strung together, suddenly articulate, as if a dam inside him had broken, letting them through. "I'm the only one who knows why. I know. I know which one of them did it. I know."

"If you do know," I said, "you ought to go to the police. Captain Malone is over at Judge Whitney's now. Why don't you go and tell him?"

"Police?" he said at last. He was almost whispering. "They wouldn't listen—they wouldn't believe me. My—my own hands aren't clean." He looked down at his hands. Then he brought his head up and half rose from the bench.

"I'll go," he said. "I'll tell. I'll pull down the palace he's built—his—his deceit."

He stopped, sinking back down on the bench, the weak flame dying as quickly as it had flared up. His face crumpled, tears ran down his cheeks.

It seemed shameful just to leave him there, hysterical and in agony, but I didn't know how to do anything else.

Monk Whitney looked at me curiously as I came up to him. "What gives?" he. demanded. "Who's your small friend?"

I couldn't speak for an instant. "That's Mr. Toplady," I said then. "I'm——"

He cut me off abruptly, instantly alert. "The man who wrote Kane the letter?"

I nodded. He took a couple of quick steps past me and stopped.

"Where is he?"

I looked back. The bench he'd been sitting on was empty. There was no trace of him anywhere.

"Who is Mr. Toplady, Monk?" I asked.

He didn't answer. He'd thrown away his cigarette, and he

stood with his brows drawn together, fumbling absently in his pocket for another. He lighted one deliberately, as if it were a process demanding his entire attention.

"Come on," he said. "Let's go eat."

We didn't stop at the Barclay or the Warwick. "We'd better steer clear of the haunts of the elite," he said.

The place we went to was down a narrow side street and up a flight of rickety steps. It obviously had been a speakeasy once, but it was quiet and empty, and the scalopini and green peppers fried in olive oil were very good, and it was pleasantly nostalgic with the iron-grille peephole in the door and the straw-covered bottles on the plate rail that had once held somebody's best china plates.

"It's none of my business," I said, when the waiter had gone back through the bamboo-and-bead curtain.

"It's certainly not," Monk said. "But what?"

"It's just that you aren't making sense," I said. "You can't act the way you did with Captain Malone and expect to get away with it."

He didn't raise his eyes from his plate. "I don't give a damn about Malone."

"Now you're being childish," I said. "Why don't you tell him where you were this afternoon?"

"Because I can't, lady," he said evenly. He looked across at me. "It's you that's not making sense. What would you do if you—well, if you were in the spot I'm in? You wouldn't expect me to shed any tears for Kane, would you? And if he hadn't got bumped off this afternoon, he'd be with the district attorney right now, and in the morning where'd my father be?"

"Do you know that?" I asked.

"That's what I've been doing today," he said quietly. "And I can't say to Malone, 'I wasn't at the Curtis Building, sir; I was out in the Whitemarsh Valley, trying to find out whether it's true my father killed his best friend, so count me out.' Can I?"

"Why, no," I said. "I guess you couldn't."

"Well, that's what I was doing. I don't know why. I mean, I don't know what difference it can make now. Except that—— Good God, I've got to know! Here that poor guy—that's what's so hard to take." He stopped for a while, thinking intently, and then looked over at me. "You kill somebody," he said abruptly. "Maybe you lost your head, maybe something happened, maybe it was an accident. Okay, you try to get away with it. Nobody wants to hang. If it can be made to look like a suicide, fine. But what I can't get away with is my father—Judge Nathaniel Whitney—being a damned hypocrite." He looked down at his plate again.

"I haven't any idea at all what you're talking about," I said.

He nodded silently. "It goes back a long way, Grace," he said, after a moment. "So long you get to thinking everybody knows. Trav's father and Laurel's father and mine were all born around the square there, and they all grew up and went to college together. Then Laurel's father went to medical school, and Trav's and mine did law. They were tops, all of them. They were respected, and honored, and honest—or that's what everybody thought. Doctor Frazier, Laurel's father, he was a wonderful guy. They don't come any better. He worked himself to death. When he died, he didn't leave a terrific lot, but enough for Laurel and her mother, with what his father had left him. They were Quakers and pretty well heeled. You know doctors don't know much about finance, and the better they are the less they know. Anyway, he left it with Travis's father, Douglas Elliot, as discretionary trustee. He was a lawyer, and he was supposed to be the soul of honor. You know. Without any of my father's dramatic flair."

He seemed to be coming to the hard part, the way he hesitated before he went on.

"Everything was fine, then, or seemed to be. Trav went to law school and came back and went in his father's office and got engaged to Elsie. At least there was a sort of family understanding—childhood sweethearts, that sort of thing. That was September, 1936. Laurel was sixteen and all set for—you know, the usual brilliant social career. Everything was beautiful, and then just overnight everything went to hell."

He'd folded his raincoat up on the seat beside him in the booth. He picked it up now and brought a small packet of papers out of the side pocket. They were tied together with a torn strip of white cloth.

"This is what happened to my handkerchief," he said. "I tore it up to tie these together. I couldn't risk losing any of them." He loosened the knot with his fork. "We've got a place out in the Whitemarsh Valley. My father keeps his old papers in a stone barn he fixed up into a library. It's a storeroom now; he doesn't go out there much any more. He had it all together—the history of the Affaire Elliot." He picked one of the clippings out and handed it across to me.

NOTED PHILADELPHIA LAWYER ENDS LIFE, the headlines said, above a picture of a handsome, black-haired, strong-faced man in his late fifties, I'd imagine.

Legal circles were shocked today to learn that Doug-las Elliot, one of the leading figures in the city's civic, social and juristic affairs, met death by his own hand in the library of his home in Delancey Place shortly before midnight last night. His body was found by his lifelong friend and associate, Judge Nathaniel Whitney. Judge Whitney, following a practice of many years' standing, had dropped in to see Mr. Elliot on his way to his home in Rittenhouse Square. A note found beside the body has not been made public. One of the most beloved and highly respected members of the bar, it is believed that the long illness and death of his wife last year must have preyed on Mr. Elliot's mind. His friends could give no other reason, as it is not believed that a heart condition, though serious, was sufficient to explain his action.

Nearly a column of Douglas Elliot's brilliant and active career followed: "He is survived by one son, Travis Elliot, at present starting his own career in his father's office in Chest-nut Street."

I put it down and looked at Monk. He was silent for a moment, his face somber and his jaw tight. Then he said:

"There wasn't a bean of Laurel's money left."

I looked at him in shocked silence.

"He'd used it all, every cent of it, speculating. You'd think he'd have learned in 1929. They said he was under such heavy expense for his wife's illness—— I don't know. They hushed it up as well as they could. That's where Travis came in." He looked down for an instant at the packet of clippings and letters. "He wasn't legally responsible. His father had the right, under the terms of the trusteeship, to use the money any way he thought best—and nobody could prove he didn't think what he was doing was the best. I never saw the letter —what was taken as the suicide note—but I understood it said he hoped Travis would do anything he could for Laurel and her mother. What I mean is, he didn't legally have to."

"And did he?" I asked.

"Did he? He turned over his father's insurance. It was only about twenty-five thousand. He sold everything they had except the Delancey Place house. He'd have sold that, but nobody lived in town then. It's only since the war and gas rationing that anybody'd be caught dead staying in. Everybody lived out on the Main Line or Chestnut Hill or in the Whitemarsh Valley, except the already dead and buried. The old business of 'Chestnut, Walnut, Spruce and Pine' was ancient history. He simply cleaned himself out and turned the money over to Laurel's mother."

It explained a lot, of course, I was thinking.

"And that's why she's supposed to be grateful to him?"

He looked at me, not understanding. "A lot of people wouldn't have done it. And that's not all he did. Every cent he made he turned over to them. His father didn't have much when it was turned into cash, and Trav wasn't making much, but he worked like a dog and lived on bread and cheese, practically. And never a peep out of him. That's what makes it so——"

He stopped again, trying to cover up how hard hit he was by all of it.

"You see," he said, "in Philadelphia, people still have the quaint idea that if you misuse money that's entrusted to you, you're no better than a common thief. If your father did it, you're the son of a common thief. If your father does it and commits suicide, it doesn't make it any better, it makes it a hell of a lot worse. Trav had damned tough going. Elsie threw him over, crack out of the box, and married Soapy Sam, or Up From Scrapple to Caviar, and all the mothers snatched their beautiful daughters out of his path—and had they been pushing them into it! It wasn't easy, Grace. It was damned hard."

"He seems to be all right now," I said.

He nodded. "Yeah. That's what I'm coming to, slowly. That's what I can't stand about my father in all this. Maybe he went over there that night, knowing his old pal had cleaned out the widow and orphan of his other old pal."

He stopped, staring down at his plate, recreating in his mind, I supposed, the scene that night eight years ago in the Elliot library when his father was passing final judgment, perhaps, on the man who was his friend.

"I don't know, Grace. That's all right, I guess. I'm not saying maybe he didn't have provocation enough. But after you kill a guy, whether he had it coming or not, you don't then take his son in and let him get the idea you're his great and noble benefactor."

There was such bitterness in his voice that it was hard to

believe it was his own father he was talking about, after the way he'd spoken the night before—before he'd heard Abigail Whitney and knew his father had killed Elliot.

"You see, Trav was crazy about his father," he went on slowly. "He just took it on the chin and shut up. The only thing he ever said was he couldn't understand his father taking that kind of out. I mean, he tried like the devil to find some excuse to explain it to himself. I know he went to his father's doctor. That was the tough part of it. If it was cancer or heart, then he could save something out of it—a decent memory. But there wasn't." He gave me a twisted kind of grin. "What I'm getting at, Grace, is my father and old Abigail. Everybody thought they were wonderful, the way they stood by. I guess one of the things that burn me up now is that one of the memories I had of my father is seeing him after the funeral. He brought Trav back to stay at our house. I can see him standing in the library with his arm around Trav's shoulder, giving him a pep talk about being captain of his soul and not letting another man's mistake warp his own life. He was wonderful—like one of the old Romans. Trav wanted to pay up and get out—go to New York or someplace where everybody didn't know him. My father wouldn't let him. He'd help him build up his practice, and so on."

The waiter took away our plates, looking pointedly at the clock.

"He did that, and he carried Trav's torch all over the place. He got everybody on his side. He saw that everybody knew Trav was paying up and knew Laurel and her mother were getting everything the guy could scrape together. So everybody pitched in, and Trav got all the breaks he deserved, and it's been swell."

"Then what are you——"

"What I'm objecting to is Trav thinking my father was doing it for his sake, for him, because he loved his father, instead of doing it to—to ease over a guilty conscience. That's what I'm objecting to. Trav thinks my father is the Number One guy of the universe. He's worked like a slave helping him, doing the dirty work on the books my father writes. He goes to see old Abigail all the time, and she could give him the money to replace what his father took without noticing it as much as if I gave a beggar a dime. Both of them, they've used him, used him all the time; and they knew all the time that the thing that was eating him was the fact

91

that his father was a suicide, taking a run-out powder instead of facing the music. They've built him up, and what for? Just to cover the fact that my father, Judge Nathaniel Whitney, is a murderer. And Abigail—that old whited sepulcher. Pretending she's bedridden——"

He took another of the clippings out of the packet and pushed it across to me.

ACCIDENT AT FUNERAL OF PROMINENT SUICIDE, it said. It was from one of the sensational tabloids. There was a picture of Abigail Whitney in a Merry Widow hat dripping with ostrich plumes that must have been in the paper's morgue for years.

FAMOUS BEAUTY'S ACCIDENT RECALLS GOSSIP LINKING HER WITH DEAD LAWYER, it went on.

Many of Philadelphia's socially elite are recalling that Abigail Whitney's elopement with her first husband, a millionaire cotton broker, was widely believed to be the result of a broken heart when Douglas Elliot married another. Her spectacular career was given a setback yesterday when she slipped getting into her limousine and sustained a broken hip. The coolness that has existed throughout each of her successive marriages between Abigail Whitney and her brother, Judge Nathaniel Whitney, is rumored to have resulted from his interference in the match that would have made her the bride of a struggling young lawyer.

"Is that true?" I asked. "I mean, about Abigail and Travis' father?"

Monk Whitney nodded. "The Whitneys, my dear madam, are a practical people. It's just as simple to fall in love with somebody with money as with somebody without money. Abigail set out to embarrass them with a *reductio ad absurdum*. And she never forgot and never forgave. She also hates Elsie for having thrown Trav over. Though actually I don't think Elsie was really in love with him before he was cleaned out."

"And what about Laurel?" I asked.

"Ah, yes," he said. "Miss Laurel Frazier. She upset the applecart completely. Her mother died at the end of her second year in college, three years after the debacle. They sold their house and moved into a little apartment in Bryn Mawr and scraped along on the interest of what Trav paid

92

back. Then Laurel quit college and said she wasn't taking anything from anybody, now that her mother was dead, and handed Trav back the principal intact. It's mounting up someplace now. Neither of them will touch it."

His voice had a kind of controlled bitterness and pain.

"And that's just some more of the same," he went on. "She's just like Trav. She came to my father six months after her mother died, and she's been there ever since, and she thinks he's done her a great favor. She thinks she's deeply indebted to him. And if Douglas Elliot had—had stayed alive, he'd have kept quiet about everything and paid them enough out of his earnings to let them live decently."

"She can't really afford to burn up a fur coat just for fun, then, can she?" I asked.

"What do you mean?"

I told him what I meant, with some warmth because of the skeptical lift of his eyebrows the minute I began.

"Look, Grace," he said. "That sounds fine—and it's phony on the face of it."

"It wasn't," I said flatly. "I was there and I saw her do it. It wasn't phony at all. She was almost frantic."

"All right," he said. "She was almost frantic if you say so. I don't doubt it. But why?"

"Why?" I said. "Good heavens, it was your handkerchief, and it had blood all over it, and she was at the Curtis Building this afternoon. I saw her come out, and that's probably where she found it; she hadn't been at your house very long."

"Okay," he said. "But I wasn't at the Curtis Building this afternoon, and don't forget it. I don't know how my handkerchief got there, if it is mine. But the point is a little different, Grace. Laurel Frazier's been with my father about five years. My father's a lawyer, and a good one, and she's nobody's fool."

"Which means——?"

"Just this," he said rather grimly: "She knew as well as I know now—and I don't train with lawyers—that Malone wasn't going to search the house. You still have to have a search warrant to search people's houses in this country, Mrs. Latham. The idea of Malone's getting out one to search Judge Nathaniel Whitney's house is crazy. If she hadn't wanted Malone to find the handkerchief, she'd have left it in her pocket and nobody'd have known the difference."

"No," I said. "I don't believe it, not for one minute. I'm

telling you. She really was frantic. She just wasn't stopping to use her head."

"She was using her head all right," he said quietly. "She got the bloodhounds hot on my trail and off somebody else's. I call that using the old bean, even if you don't."

I looked at him blankly.

"You're being the dope this time, Grace. I know it sounds lovely, but it just ain't so. Laurel Frazier wouldn't go two feet out of her way to save me from the bottomless pit. I've known her all her life. She's got the temper of a redheaded hornet and she thinks I'm a louse. Maybe she's right. I was raising a lot of hell when she came to work for my father, and she got in on all of it. She kept his checkbook, and she used to add postscripts to his—his paternal remonstrances that would take the back hair off an armadillo."

"They haven't got back hair," I said.

"Whatever they've got, then. And it's all okay. She thought I was a pain in the neck to my father, and after the Affaire Elliot and her mother's death, my father meant security to her, and everything her father had meant, and she went all out. She's just nuts about him. There's nothing she wouldn't do for him. And that's why I don't think she ought to be bamboozled into marrying Trav. Don't get me wrong, Grace; he's a swell guy; they don't come any better. But that gal's got something. If she was really in love with a guy, she'd burn her coat and her hands and she'd burn that hair of hers off to help him out of a jam. But she wouldn't do it for me. Not that baby."

He grinned at me suddenly across the table.

"There I go," he said. "You've probably read a book about Psychology for the Man in the Street, and you figure I'm always harping on who she doesn't love and shouldn't marry because I'm in love with her myself and don't know it. And you're wrong. What I'd like to do is break her neck. And I'd like to know who she's rigging me up for. I'd also like to know what she was doing over at the Curtis Building this afternoon."

I was looking at him with bewilderment. "You haven't heard about the manuscript?"

"What manuscript?"

"The profile of your father, Myron's piece. It's gone, disappeared from the composing room of the *Post* this noon."

He was looking at me blankly.

"Before Myron was killed," I went on. "The work-sheet

number or whatever they call it was right by his body. But the script wasn't. It was taken out of the monotype keyboard basket while the foreman was out to lunch. And the knife he was killed with came from the cutting-down bench in the electrotyping division."

He was looking steadily at me. "Go on."

I went on. I told him the whole business. At the end, I went back and told him about the ghost of Benjamin Franklin. I thought I was adding a light touch that would relieve for a moment the staggering effect of the rest of it, but I was wrong.

"Good God," he said, his voice little more than a whisper.

"And, Monk, there's one other thing I think you ought to know. Laurel knows about your father."

His face turned an odd sort of flat color, as if that was more of a shock than the rest of it had been.

"She doesn't know it was Douglas Elliot—at least, I don't believe she does. All she knows is he killed a man. Your aunt told her deliberately, to try to push her into marrying Myron Kane, to get that document back. That's what made her call up Myron at Travis' last night after your father had left, when you started throwing your weight about."

He sat there silently, doing a lot of adding and subtracting in his own head, I imagined, out of a background that I didn't know anything about.

"Well, the little fool," he said then. His voice was hardly audible. "The poor, crazy little fool." He picked up the packet of papers and stuck them into his pocket. "Come on, let's get out of here." He picked up his raincoat and got out of the booth.

"What about the check?" I asked. "It's still a civilian custom."

He shouted for the waiter through the beaded curtain. The man came running in, looking as if he'd been asleep, as he probably had. He had to go back after the bill, and then he had to go back after some change.

"Sit down," I said. "He's waited long enough for us. Anyway, there's something I want to know."

He sat down impatiently on the edge of the booth.

"Who is Mr. Toplady?" I said. "And what goes on about him and Myron and your——" I didn't know whether to say "your father" or "your aunt," so I said, "your family?"

His impatience with the agitated waiter evaporated immediately. "Toplady?" He looked at me as if he had never heard the name before and couldn't possibly imagine what I was talking about.

"Yes," I said, "Mr. Toplady. He writes letters and haunts benches, and he doesn't turn up at his bank to keep an appointment with a representative of the Secretary of the Treasury. You know, Mr. Toplady."

He looked at me with complete imperturbability. "Mr. Toplady," he said. "Sorry, haven't the faintest idea. Don't know the guy. If that's really his name, he ought to change it. Imagine being stuck with a moniker like that all your life. Ready?"

At the foot of the rickety steps, he stopped. "What do you mean, not keeping an appointment with a representative of the Secretary of the Treasury?"

"Just that," I said, a little annoyed, the shadowy figure of Mr. Toplady back in my mind again—his haggard face and his sudden futile agony and despair. "He was supposed to meet Colonel Primrose this morning for a private showing of a movie about somebody's back income tax, with a canceled check as the heroine. And he didn't show."

He lost interest immediately. "Oh," he said. "Let's walk, shall we? Or do you want a taxi?"

"I'll have a taxi," I said. The streets were as deserted as a graveyard at midnight.

"I'd like to walk too," Monk said.

We turned into Locust Street and went along back toward Rittenhouse Square. At 17th he stopped and looked across the street at the brightly lighted windows of the old Yarnall house on the corner opposite the Warwick. A band was playing, and the couples dancing, laughing, past the windows of the handsome ballroom weren't much different from the ones I remembered there, except that the men were all in uniform. The painted murals were covered with panels with big blue stars painted on them. It was the gayest spot I'd seen in Philadelphia. We stood like a couple of orphans in the storm, watching them through the windows. I didn't realize what Monk was looking for until he gave up and we started on across the street. He looked back at the 17th Street entrance. A crowd of youngsters in uniform piling noisily in at the door moved aside to let a man in civilian clothes come out. It was Travis Elliot.

Monk Whitney quickened his pace, but Travis had already spotted us and called out. We stopped and waited.

"I just took Laurel over," Travis said, coming up to us. "I

sure wish this war would get over; I never see her any more. She's there all the time. Cook, bottle washer, telephone girl, taxi dancer and everything else. She's a hostess tonight, and they're standing in line. I guess she won't feel much like dancing."

He broke off abruptly, a little embarrassed. He'd obviously been talking fast, I thought, to avoid any reference to the late unpleasantness.

"They do a swell job there, Mrs. Latham," he went on hurriedly. "The organization that runs this service club's been going since 1917. They never disbanded. They had over three quarters of a million men in their old quarters in the last war and they're going way over that here. It's a beautiful house. They've got a sun deck on the roof and a laundry in the basement, with a pool table in the next room, so you don't have to waste any time while your shirt's in the drier. They've got the snappiest bunch of gals you've ever seen."

"I guess I'll resign my commission," Monk said.

It was intended to be funny, I suppose, but we fell into a gulf of embarrassed silence for a few moments.

"Unless the Marine Corps does it for me," Monk said then. "Well, go ahead. Say it. You might as well."

"All right, I will," Travis said coolly. "I don't see why the devil you had to get Malone's back up the way you did. If you want to talk about it."

"Why not?" Monk inquired. "There's no use pretending nothing's happened."

"It seems to me we ought to sort of——"

"Get together on a story?"

Travis glanced at him curiously. "Not at all," he said. "That isn't what I mean. I don't think you ought to go around shooting off your mouth until you find out what's going on. Let me offer you the example of your brother-in-law."

"What's Soapy Sam done?" Monk's tone was alert and interested.

"He's got in touch with his lawyers. To the end that, one, he's established an alibi for himself, and two, he's offered a five-thousand-dollar reward for the return of the manuscript 'purportedly'—I quote—'stolen from the composing room of The Curtis Publishing Company Building.'"

"Dead or alive, I suppose," Monk said. "What does he mean, 'purportedly'?"

"You've got me, unless he means 'purportedly,'" Travis

97

said. "But, boy, he certainly went to town. He wanted to offer another thousand bucks for the identification of someone purportedly Benjamin Franklin seen hanging around the place, but the judge stopped him."

We'd come to the 19th Street side of the square. The Whitney houses, side by side, pink paint and mellow brownstone, were dark behind drawn curtains, except for the dimly lit panels of light through the front doors.

"Where is the judge now?" Monk asked abruptly.

"Home," Travis said. "A couple of people from the *Post* are there, and the district attorney. Myron was supposed to have dinner with him tonight, you remember. Colonel Primrose is there, and they expected Malone back when I left with Laurel. They were asking for you, so if you want to look as if you aren't ducking something, I'd advise you to come on up. Aunt Abby asked me to stand by for her, though I don't know where she figures she comes in. Her alibi—speaking about alibis—is certainly foolproof, unless you believe in miracles."

"Or ghosts," Monk said. He turned to me. "Do you want to come?"

"No," I said. "I definitely do not."

I said good night and went up Abigail Whitney's steps.

I waited there until I heard the door of the brownstone house close behind Monk and Travis, and then I turned around and looked carefully over as much of the square as I could see. It was so empty that if Mr. Albert Toplady had returned to take up his ominous vigil again I couldn't possibly have missed him. A moment later I wasn't quite so sure. A large square black object that I'd taken for a granite monument started to move, and I recognized the heroic proportions of Sgt. Phineas T. Buck. He was coming across the street, and he wasn't coming to speak to me, but I went back down the steps, so he could hardly avoid it.

He took it like a soldier and a stoic. "Something off-color, ma'am?"

"No," I said. "I was just wondering what you were doing out there."

Even in the dark, I could see his face turn slowly to a sort of tarnished copper.

"The colonel wanted to make sure you got in okay, ma'am," he said.

"Oh, all right," I said, and started up the stairs again, always glad to co-operate.

Sergeant Buck cleared his throat. It sounded like a foghorn doubling in brass. It meant he had something more to say, so I turned back.

"If you run into the little lady, ma'am, tell her she don't need to worry none."

"I'll tell her," I said.

"But tell her she'd ought to try to clarify her skirts, ma'am," he added very seriously.

It disturbed me a little. Usually, when Sergeant Buck extended the protection of his rock-ribbed wing, it was with an entirely mistaken if complete conviction of innocence indirectly involved with the clarification of skirts. Or so Colonel Primrose always said.

I nodded.

"And now if you'll go to bed, ma'am," he said patiently, "I got work to do. No offense meant, ma'am," he added hastily, as if his own skirts might do with a bit of clarifying.

"None taken, sergeant," I said. "Good night."

He waited on the curb until the door opened. I caught a glimpse of him as I went in, turning his head and spitting over the hood of Travis' car. As far as Sergeant Buck was concerned, I was in the finished-business basket for the night.

Closing the front door of Abigail Whitney's house was not, however, synonymous with getting directly to bed. I still had the second-floor gantlet to run, and I saw, as soon as I reached the mirror on the stairs, that it was going to be a delaying task. Mrs. Whitney's door was open, her light was on, and she was sitting up in her yellow cushions like a crafty old spider in the middle of her web.

"Come in, Dear Child," she called as I passed the shell recess in the upper hall.

I went in. She was sitting up against her cushions all wrapped up in soft fluffy marabou, and looked grotesquely like an amiable old buzzard who'd eaten a gosling, except for its downy jacket, which she was now wearing. Her eyes were alert and very bright, and I wondered how she managed to keep herself in bed when she was as excited as she plainly was. She tried to relax as I came into the room, and appear Interested But Detached.

"Dear Child," she said, "I must Tell you. The Police have been here. And Colonel Primrose. They are Delightful People; they couldn't have been More Charming."

"I'm sure they couldn't," I said.

And I imagined they were. I could see them, all of them,

practically turning handsprings, trying not to disturb the invalid in her sanctuary more than they could help.

"But Captain Malone is a very Strange Man, Dear Child," she said. "I'm sure if the taxpayers Really Knew——"

"Really knew what?" I asked blankly.

"Well, Dear Child," she said. "Surely it isn't customary for the Police to go to Fancy-Dress Balls when they're investigating murders. Or is it? I'm sure you're much more Familiar with their Procedure than I."

"I don't know what you mean, Mrs. Whitney," I said.

"Well, it's rather awkward, to be sure," she said, her voice going vaguely off. "I suppose it was Unfortunate, Really. But, you see, he came with his valise, and my man, whose hearing is most imperfect, mistook him for a guest, and laid out his things in the guest room downstairs. And would you realize, Dear Child, what he had in his bag?"

I shook my head and waited, for some reason holding my breath a little.

"Well, I've told you, Dear Child. It was a masquerade costume. Of an Eighteenth-Century Quaker gentleman. I would assume he was going as Benjamin Franklin. But it's most Extraordinary, carrying it around with him while he's investigating crime. But the most extraordinary thing, my dear; it had Blood On It." She looked at me with bland open blue eyes. "You would have thought," she said, "that he would have been grateful to my man for cleaning it off—as any well-trained servant would do. But not at all. Dear Child, you won't believe it, but he was Livid—Absolutely Livid."

10

It was bootless, of course, to try to speculate on where Captain Malone had found the clothes that Benjamin Franklin had worn and got blood on, especially with no help from Abigail Whitney. Having said he was livid at finding them neatly cleaned and pressed, she promptly dismissed both the subject and me.

"You may leave the door open, Dear Child," she said, "I find the atmosphere of Philadelphia rather Oppressive at Times. But many people do, of course."

I was glad to get up to my room and leave the door closed. And I had the feeling that if Sergeant Buck could forget his distaste of me sufficiently to ask me to tell Laurel she didn't have to worry, it was of considerable importance. She had plenty to worry about already, and if, in the long night ahead of her, there was one point on which she could be at rest, it would be a good thing to let her know about it.

The telephone was still plugged in and on my bedside table. I looked up the United Service Club and dialed the number. A pleasant voice answered. I asked if I could speak to Miss Laurel Frazier.

"I'm sorry," the woman said. "Miss Frazier wasn't feeling very well, so she went home. She didn't stay but a moment. If you'll wait, I have her number here."

After I had dialed it and waited, hearing the periodic burr at the other end of the line, I looked her name up in the phone book, wondering where she lived when she wasn't at the brownstone house next door. It was a number on Locust Street between 17th and 18th, which meant it was just across the square, a stone's throw from the club. I put down the phone and dialed again, just to make sure, but there was still no answer. She had probably gone back to Judge Whitney's, I thought. Nevertheless, I tried her number again after I'd got ready for bed and put the windows up. Wherever she was, she wasn't at home.

I turned off the light and lay there. It was hard to relax enough to go to sleep, wondering what was going on next door, and wondering also whether my hostess was prowling around the house. Finally the meeting next door broke up. I could hear men's voices, and then their feet on the brownstone steps, and a succession of car doors slamming and motors turning on. The sounds died gradually away, leaving the street silent for a few moments.

Then I heard the door close again and Travis Elliot speaking. "I guess I'll go over to the club and pick Laurel up."

"I'll come along, if you don't mind." I recognized Monk's voice. "I need some fresh air."

"Sure, come on," Travis said. "We'll have a chance to talk."

I wondered first whether Monk Whitney was actually fooling himself that it was fresh air he wanted, and then whether Travis Elliot would have agreed with as much readiness if he'd pondered that book Monk had been talking about. I also wondered whether Monk had got around to telling Travis, as friend and well-wisher, that Laurel Frazier wasn't the girl for him to marry. If he weren't so determined that Psychology for the Man in the Street didn't apply to him, he'd have a better chance, it seemed to me, than he appeared to have now. He'd probably have to wait until he woke up some morning in a foxhole somewhere thousands of miles from home, the way he'd waked up out in the Pacific realizing how much his father meant to him. And if Laurel had married Travis before he came back, it would be too late. She'd be too loyal and too stubborn—and so would he— to admit there'd been a mistake. I heard their footsteps echoing and fading out across the square, and then the faint faraway rhythm of dance music.

Then I awoke with sudden and appalling clarity. Judge Nathaniel Whitney was speaking. It was his voice that woke me up, right there in the room.

"I am here. What else do you want me to do?"

I sat up, the cold, deliberative force of his voice in my ears robbing me of all power to move or to speak to him. But I couldn't speak to him or see him; he wasn't there. A sudden sort of panic seized me, and I grabbed at my dressing gown and put it around my shoulders and switched on the light.

The room was quite empty. I looked around it blankly, and then I got up and went over to the closet door and opened it. A light came on in the ceiling, but all it showed was the cedar lining and cedar shelves built in against the wall and covered with yellow rosebud chintz. Judge Whitney was certainly not lurking anywhere in there.

It could have been a dream, I thought, closing the door again, but I hadn't been dreaming up to that time, as far as I knew, and there was no dream content mixed up with what I remembered.

The words and the tone of Judge Whitney's voice were still vividly clear in my mind. "I am here. What else do you want me to do?"

It might have been the jinni in the *Arabian Nights*, coming at the call of the lamp but rebuking Aladdin for his presumptuous demands. That was precisely what it sounded like, with the "else" definitely emphasized.

I sat on the edge of the bed, looking around—I couldn't quite bring myself to look under it—half expecting I'd still find him or that he'd go on and say something else. But that was that. The room and the house and everything around me was as silent as the grave. I decided I must be getting psychic as a result of all the ghosts around, and then I decided that was nonsense. I had heard Judge Whitney. I hadn't imagined it at all.

I turned out the light and went over to the window and looked out into the square, just to get a sense of other people, and to get out of my mind, so I could go to bed again and go to sleep, a feeling that I was a kind of prisoner cooped up in the third floor of a madhouse. I wasn't exactly frightened, but I'd have been pleased to see Sergeant Buck standing down there or even Mr. Albert Toplady—or even the squirrel, for that matter. Actually, the person I saw was none of them. It was Judge Whitney.

I'd just started to go back to bed when I heard a sound and looked down into the street. There was a widening oblong of light as the door of the brownstone house opened and a heavy shadow elongated against it. It closed then, and I saw Judge Whitney come out, putting on his hat. He stopped halfway down the steps and glanced up at Abigail's window. I thought for an instant that he might be trying to see whether she was still awake and watching in her mirror, and then I saw that it was quite the contrary. He was holding his cigar lighter up much longer than was necessary to light his cigar, looking up at her mirror, his face illuminated there, so that if she was watching at all, she wouldn't fail to see him. Then he snapped off the lighter and went on down the steps and along 19th Street toward Walnut.

"I am here. What else do you want me to do?" I could hear the words again. It was his sister Abigail he was talking to, and in some way I didn't know about, I'd overheard it. I had a sudden intuitive certainty of it as clear as the words themselves had been. He'd been downstairs, talking to her again as he'd been the night before. How he'd got there or got back to his own house—— That dilemma vanished as I heard the sound of hurrying feet out in the square.

I looked quickly across. For a moment I couldn't see anyone, though the steps on the paved walk were coming closer. Then a small dark figure materialized out of the shadows full into the light, and I saw Mr. Albert Toplady again. He was coming from the Locust Street end of the square and headed toward the pink house, I thought, drawing back from the window sill. He was looking up at it, but before he came to the curb across the street, he changed his course and went to the brownstone house. At the bottom step he hesitated, but only for a second, and went up and rang the bell.

It seemed to me a very long time before I heard the door open and the muffled sound of voices. They weren't muffled long—at least one of them wasn't.

The Irish maid's Irish rose, and her voice with it. ". . . I'm tellin' you it's no decent hour for you to come disturbin' the judge! You can come back in the mornin', and see you keep a civil tongue in your head when you do!"

The door slammed shut emphatically. In a moment, Mr. Toplady came slowly down the steps and went off—if he had known it—following Judge Whitney toward Walnut Street, a forlorn figure, his brief candle of courage snuffed rudely out.

I don't know at what point it was during the night that it came into my head that Judge Whitney was going on some errand for his sister. That "What else do you want me to do?" implied, of course, that he had already done something. If it had been anybody but Judge Whitney, it might have occurred to me that what he had done had been the little matter of chopping Myron Kane. But that was an absurdity that even I boggled at.

11

One of the things about men is that they're never around when you need them. I went downstairs the next morning at a quarter to nine, my date with Captain Malone at the Second Detective Division, 12th and Pine, weighing a little heavily on my mind. I'd sort of taken it for granted that Colonel Primrose wouldn't let me go alone, but I hadn't had any word from him since he left Abigail's before Laurel tried to burn Monk's handkerchief. I couldn't exactly blame him, considering that I'd been anything but helpful—and not reasonable, but when has any woman been reasonable? Nor was there any reason I shouldn't go alone. A police station is probably the safest and most respectable place in the world.

Nevertheless, I thought Colonel Primrose was playing me a dirty trick, and I was glad when Abigail called me as I came downstairs, so I'd have a chance to tell somebody so. She was sitting up in her swan's bed, her breakfast tray still across her lap, her henna hair still done up in aluminum curlers, which looked very funny above her fancy lace and sea-green quilted-satin bed jacket. It was surprising, too, because Travis Elliot was there, having a cup of coffee with her, and I'd have thought her vanity would have at least demanded a frilly handkerchief over the curlers if there was a man around.

"What are you Doing out at This Hour, Dear Child?" she demanded. From her surprised incredulity, you'd have thought it was a quarter past five.

"It's a command invitation from Captain Malone," I explained. "I thought Colonel Primrose would be here to escort me, but I expect he's down at the Quaker Trust Company doing his job for Mr. Morgenthau."

Abigail put her chocolate cup down. "Are you suggesting that you're going alone, Dear Child?" she said. "To a Police Station?"

The polite horror in her voice put the whole thing in its proper perspective at once.

"Surely," I said. "Why not?"

"I've never Heard of Such a Thing," she said. "Never. And you're doing Nothing of the Sort. . . . Get up, Travis. Get up at once. You'll Go With Her, Dear Boy. You should, anyway. My husbands were all very Intelligent and Far-Seeing men, and there was only one point on which they were in Unanimous Agreement. That was that one should never talk without his Lawyer Present. While they never went to Police Stations, I'm very Sure if they had they wouldn't have dreamed of going without Legal Support."

Travis put down his cup and got up obediently. He was trying not to laugh. "I don't think it's as dangerous as all that, Aunt Abby," he said. "But I'll be glad to go along if Mrs. Latham would like to have me."

"You'll go whether she likes it or not, Dear Boy," Abigail said. "I've had one of my guests murdered. I don't intend to have the other thrown into prison by that astonishing man who carries Bloody Clothes around in Satchels."

"Isn't she wonderful?" Travis said. "Come on. I've got my car out here." We went out the front door and down the steps. "What I'd like to know is what this is she's saying about Malone's fancy dress. I'd say Malone hasn't had a fancy dress since he wore a sheet on Halloween."

"Didn't they talk about it last night?"

He shook his head, looking inquiringly at me.

"About Benjamin Franklin's ghost turning up at the Curtis Building yesterday when Myron was—was murdered?"

He'd put the key in the lock. He turned and looked at me. "You don't think you ought to go back to bed for an hour or two?" he asked with a grin. "Or am I crazy?"

"It's someone else, I believe," I said. "Captain Malone thought it was the watchman at the reception desk—he was the one who saw the ghost. Now that he's found the raiments and they had blood on them, I gather, I guess he's decided the ghost was real enough."

He shook his head.

"Well, I don't know what it means either," I said. "But apparently the watchman wasn't making it up entirely."

As he opened the car door, the door of the brownstone house opened and Monk came out. He was in uniform, and looked very snappy except for the lined patches under his eyes.

He came over to us. "Where you guys going?"

"I'm taking Mrs. Latham to the police station for Aunt Abby," Travis said.

Monk looked quickly at me. "Twelfth and Pine?"

I nodded.

"Give me a lift then, will you, Trav? I got a summons this morning too. I was going to ask if you thought you ought to go along, and then I thought I'd let them make the first move."

"What does the judge think?"

They had both become serious all of a sudden.

"I don't know," Monk answered shortly. "I haven't seen him since last night."

"Maybe we'd better——"

At that moment a taxi came to a stop at the curb. I thought for a moment, seeing Sergeant Buck in it, that his colonel was there, too, but he wasn't. Sergeant Buck got out, started toward the pink house, saw the three of us standing there, and came toward us. He advanced to within six paces, came to a formal halt, and gave the impression of not actually but still, in effect, saluting a commissioned officer.

"My orders, sir, were to accompany the lady to the police station at Twelfth and Pine," he said. "Be there at nine-thirty, sir."

Monk looked inquiringly at me.

"I'm going with Major Whitney and Mr. Elliot, sergeant," I said. "You tell Colonel Primrose."

Sergeant Buck didn't actually take me by the scruff of the neck and put me into his taxi, but he got in himself, and when we turned out of Rittenhouse Square, he and the taxi were just behind us.

"What am I going to tell Captain Malone?" I asked.

"Just tell what happened," Travis said with a shrug. "Don't get yourself out on a limb. Malone's a right sort of guy."

"Shall I tell him about Mr. Toplady's letter to Myron?"

We were sitting together in the front seat, Monk on my right. He gave me a sort of dig with his elbow.

"Of course, if you think it's got anything to do with it," Travis said.

"I might as well, I guess. Colonel Primrose will see him at the bank and tell him himself, probably."

"I should think you could skip it," Monk said shortly.

"We don't want to see the judge—I mean, he's got political enemies who'd give their eyeteeth to get anything they could use. Anyway, if I'm going to be your counsel, I don't want to see Malone get you tied up in anything."

"We don't know the letter had anything to do with it," Monk said stubbornly.

"Well, we're not defending Toplady. It might be a good idea to put Malone on his trail."

"I don't want to do that," I said. "I feel very sorry for him, someway."

Travis smiled at me. "That's the woman for you. Have you ever heard of a commodity called Justice?"

Monk Whitney stared out the window, his jaw tightening. He was thinking, I supposed, of a commodity called Justice that hadn't been weighed out properly once before.

"I'd suggest, since this is a beginning anyway," Travis said, "that you don't volunteer any information. Just answer his questions and to hell with it. I don't see what you're worrying about."

He didn't, of course. Only Monk and I saw.

"The point is, when you start leaving things out, everybody leaves out something different and puts in what somebody else left out. Malone's a smart cooky. Don't let him fool you that he's just a father confessor and we all hate crime. He loves it."

He turned down 12th and over to Pine. It was a one-way street with shiny red patrol cars parked on both sides. The gaunt, shabby old building swarmed with activity.

We went up steps into a big barn of a room that had a magistrate's bench along the wall facing the door and a lot of minor offenders waiting trial. There was an interested, curious silence as we came in. Travis said, "Captain Malone," and we were ushered through a door at the left, up wooden stairs to the second floor, and along the corridor.

There was considerable activity up here too. They couldn't find the key to the stand-up room, it appeared. Then an officer bellowed that the key to the stand-up room was in the cigar box in somebody's desk. We were then conducted into a big room where there was a fenced-off row of chairs in front of the windows overlooking the street.

In the row of chairs was a row of editors of *The Saturday Evening Post*—at least there were two of them and the man from the reception desk, the man who had seen Benjamin Franklin. He was the most pleased looking of the three. I supposed, with absolutely everybody doubting his veracity, if not his sanity, he had reason to be. He also had an air of mildly beaming importance. I wondered for an instant if Captain Malone was planning a line-up of people dressed like Benjamin Franklin for him to look over. But that seemed a rather elaborate tour de force, and if Monk and both of the editors there were to be in the line-up, they'd have to have widely assorted sizes of breeches, stockings and coats.

Actually, Monk and one of the editors there could have worn the same clothes. They were both six feet tall and as brawny as a couple of stevedores. The other editor was Fred Nelson, the man who writes the *Post* editorials that *PM* doesn't like. He looked very nervous indeed. He kept hunting for something in every pocket, pulling out letters and clippings, and mumbling, "I wondered where that was," and putting them back where he'd forget them again, never seeing the pencil right on the arm of his chair till after he'd borrowed one from Pete Martin. It would have been amusing if a detective hadn't been watching him out of the corner of his eye; not realizing, I imagined, that Mr. Nelson's secretary spent her days finding things for him and her nights worrying about whether he'd lose his brief case on the way to the office from St. David's on the Main Line.

I thought Mr. Pete Martin looked nervous, too, but with a difference. He had bright blue eyes that could no doubt already see the lead of an article that, not being Pete Martin, I wouldn't have the temerity to put in words for him. He was hunched down in his chair, his hands stuck in the pockets of his big camel's-hair overcoat, his face slightly red, his grayish hair parted in the middle and somewhat disheveled.

No one would ever have taken either of them for a writer or editor, I thought. Mr. Nelson might have been up on a charge of being a bookie who had seen calmer days. Mr. Martin could have been a professional fullback who'd left the training table for cakes and ale. I don't mean to imply for an instant, of course, that the fact they could easily have been taken for confidence men or horse dopers wasn't entirely due to their immediate environment. All I mean is that if you get people into a police-station anteroom, they just naturally look as if it was surprising that they hadn't been picked up a long time before. I'm sure that's the way I looked, because I felt guiltier by the moment as I sat there waiting, and Monk too. It's the way decent people look in the hands of the law.

The sharp contrast to all the rest of us was Travis, a professional, of course, and used to the machinations of the law, and, a moment later, Mr. Samuel Phelps, who came in with an immaculate respectability and a confidence in himself as a taxpayer who hired these people that made the rest of us look guiltier than hell, if I may be allowed language not permitted in police stations when ladies are present.

The sight of Monk Whitney sitting against the window ledge behind me caused a momentary ripple on the surface of Sam's self-esteem, but it was only momentary.

"How do you do, Mrs. Latham," he said. "Hello, Travis . . . Monk." He went over to the detective at the railed-in desk. "I am Samuel Phelps," he said. "I've got a busy day. Let Captain Malone know I'm here at once, please."

"He's busy right now," the detective said. "Will you take your place? We'll let him know you're here."

Sam came back. "Have you heard anything yet this morning?" he asked Travis.

"No. I just came for the ride."

At that moment one of the detectives signalled the man who'd seen Benjamin Franklin, and he went in through a railed-off passage and into a back room. Sam frowned and looked at his watch.

"I've got to telephone the office," Travis Elliot said. "If you'll excuse me a minute. It looks like we're all going to be here a while."

He went out and downstairs. I saw Sergeant Buck move up where he could keep an eye on us.

"Mrs. Latham!"

I started as my name was called, and got up, dropped my bag and gloves, and caught my last pair of nylon stockings on a piece of wire my chair had been repaired with. If it had been a tactical delaying action instead of congenital awkwardness, it would have been brilliant, because it took long enough for me to gather up my truck for Travis to reappear in time to go in with me. I could see the detective watching me make a mental note: *Latham—nervous when called.*

The only satisfaction I had, going in, was that it annoyed Sam.

"I have an important engagement at ten-fifteen," he said.

Fred Nelson's lower jaw worked a little sideways. "It's with Captain Malone, mister," he said.

12

Captain Malone was in a room as big as a hall closet. He got up from his seat behind the desk for an inch or so, and sat down again, looking at Travis with a faint smile.

"Hullo there, Elliot," he said affably. "Mrs. Latham doesn't trust us in Philadelphia, I guess."

Travis grinned back at him. "Mrs. Whitney's idea," he said. "You outraged her so, carrying your disguise around, she wouldn't let Mrs. Latham come alone."

"Oh, you mean this."

Captain Malone reached down by the side of his chair and took up a satchel. He brought out a suit of brown Colonial clothes—knee breeches and coat, freshly laundered white stock and tan waistcoat. He put it on the desk.

"What's the butler's name?" he inquired grimly.

Travis thought. "Beppo? That's not his name. It's Tchickvinski or something."

"Well, if you can make him hear you, tell him I'm laying for him." Captain Malone gave us a sour smile. "There was blood all over this. My wife wants me to find out how he did it. Not a trace left."

"Where did you find this suit, captain?" I asked.

He thought it over a moment. "I don't know any reason I shouldn't tell you," he said deliberately. "It was stuffed down in a filing cabinet in the office of one of the editors of *The Saturday Evening Post*. Mr. Frederic Nelson's office on the fifth floor of the Curtis Building. Behind a lot of old *Racing Forms* and *Congressional Records*. The index card on the outside said Grade Labeling. I guess Mr. Nelson's got some kind of private system. Anyway, that's where I found it."

"Oh," I said.

"Where'd you think I found it?" he asked pleasantly.

"I didn't know at all," I said. "I just wondered." But I was

111

aware that my "Oh" had a relief in it that I had to be careful not to repeat.

"Well, sit down, both of you," he said. "Clear those papers off the end of the table, Elliot. Can you perch there?" He turned back to me. "Mrs. Whitney tells me Kane came to her on your recommendation, Mrs. Latham."

"Not exactly," I said. "He asked me for an introduction, but he went ahead without it."

"Why didn't you give it to him?"

I didn't like to say because I hadn't seen Abigail Whitney since I'd week-ended in Philadelphia before I was married or that I wouldn't have given Myron Kane an introduction as a house guest to my worst enemy. Fortunately I could still tell the legal truth.

"I was away when he wrote and asked me for it, and when I got home and got his note, he was already installed without it."

"He was a pretty good friend of yours?"

"I've known him four or five years."

"You didn't come up to Mrs. Whitney's just to be——"

I saw what he meant, and I must have flushed the color of a cabbage rose. It was true, in a sense, but not in the sense he meant.

I looked at Travis. We both of us saw what a beautiful chance it was to keep a rattling skeleton quietly in the closet and not have to drag it out by admitting the real reason. I smiled.

"Well," I said, "I wouldn't have come, probably, if he hadn't been there."

I trust heaven will forgive me. And I didn't stop to think where it would lead.

"You're a widow, aren't you?" Captain Malone said benevolently. "Were you—I mean, you weren't——"

Travis helped him out, "You weren't planning to marry Myron, were you?"

"Oh, no, indeed," I said. "I'm forty-one. I'd hardly marry Myron."

"Kane was forty-two. You'd have to have a better reason than that."

I would never have thought of Myron, with his perennial glamour, as that old.

Captain Malone looked at me intently over the top of his glasses. I don't believe he believed a word I'd said. He opened his desk drawer slowly. The newspaper-wrapped package with Monk's handkerchief in it was untied already. He took it out carefully and put it on the desk.

"Where did Miss Frazier get this, Mrs. Latham?"

"I haven't the faintest idea. Why don't you ask her?"

"I have, and she refuses to say."

He smoothed out what was left of the handkerchief. The cloth was scorched yellow, but the corner where the monogram was embroidered was intact. I've never been much good at cryptograms, and most fancy monograms defeat me with all their curling decoration, but I could see the *W* without any trouble, and the *M*, and a *T* that looked upside down to me. The bloodstains had turned dark brown.

It was a little awkward, actually, with Travis sitting perched on the table looking at it too. I wasn't sure how he'd feel about the gal he was going to marry practically burning herself alive for another man.

"If you good people would be frank about these things, you'd save me time and yourselves trouble," Captain Malone said. "Did you ever hear Kane mention any trouble he was having, Mrs. Latham? With any of the editors of the *Post*, for instance?"

I shook my head. "No. But of course he was a prima donna."

He caught me up quickly on that. "Kane was a prima donna?"

"Top-flight, I'd say."

He looked at me for a moment. Then he said, "Thank you, Mrs. Latham. I'll have to ask you to stay around town. There'll probably be a point or two you'll be able to help me on."

Travis got down from his perch. "I'll be glad to produce her for you any time."

Captain Malone gave him a sour smile. "Thanks."

"And by the way, Monk Whitney's a client of mine, too, Malone," Travis said. "I hope you don't mind if I stick around."

Malone looked at him patiently. "Okay. Stick around." He turned to me. "You can go out this way, Mrs. Latham."

I saw then why they wanted the key to the stand-up room. It was a way into the corridor that kept people from seeing each other again after one and before the others had seen Captain Malone.

I heard, "Mr. Martin, please," as I went out, Travis following me. I couldn't hear what Sam said.

"Don't think he's through with you," Travis said to me under his breath. "He hasn't begun." Then he said in his normal tone, "Can you get home all right? I'll take you downstairs. Where's Man Mountain Buck got to?"

Downstairs the desk sergeant leaned out of his cage at the left of the door and said, "You the lady knows Mr. Buck?"

I nodded. It's one of those anomalies I'm always conscious of. I don't really know Sergeant Buck at all.

"He said to tell you he was taking a young lady home. Red-haired girl. Pretty."

Travis Elliot and I looked at each other. "Miss Frazier?" he asked.

"Don't know her name. Captain had her up there." He went back to his paper work.

A taxi was just letting out Bob Fuoss and Erd Brandt from *The Saturday Evening Post* in front of the building. Apparently Captain Malone was dragging in the editors two by two.

Travis got me their cab. "I wish she'd told me she was coming over. She must have known about it when we saw her about midnight."

When I demanded, "Midnight?" I must have said it as if I thought everybody in Philadelphia was in bed by nine-fifteen.

"Sure. Monk and I went over to the Service Club and got her."

"I thought she went home early."

I wished I hadn't said it, because if she'd gone back she obviously didn't want him to know she'd left. Him or somebody.

"She always stays till they shut up shop," he said. "I'd better go call her."

He glanced up at the window over the door. Monk's large marine-clad back was still framed in it. The taxi stopped in front of Judge Whitney's, behind a black sedan just pulling up in front by the pink house ahead of us.

The driver leaned forward. "Look, lady. Ain't that cute?"

I leaned forward too. "Oh," I said. "He always does that."

It was the squirrel. He was hobbling arthritically down the steps with a walnut in his mouth. He looked up the street for traffic, and scooted as fast as he could across to his tree.

The driver got out and opened the door. A man was leaving the black sedan ahead of us. He went up Mrs. Whitney's steps.

"Maybe he'll do it again," I said as I paid my fare. "He comes over every time anybody goes up to the door."

"Sure enough?" the driver said.

He gave me my change, and we stood a minute watching the squirrel get up to the top step and sit up with his paws out.

The driver's face fell suddenly. "Aw, gee! They didn't give him one."

The door closed and the man was coming back down, sticking his pencil back in his pocket. He had an aluminum-backed board in his hand and he went whistling back to his car. The squirrel came down, twitching his patchy tail with annoyance. I noticed a sign on the windshield of the sedan as I passed it: U. S. MAIL SPECIAL DELIVERY. I quickened my steps, thinking it might possibly be for me. The squirrel dashed back, but he was disappointed again, because it was Elsie Phelps who opened the door. She didn't have a walnut, and she probably didn't believe in begging anyway.

"Oh, hello," she said.

She had a brown Manila envelope folded under her arm. She didn't quite say "Are you still here?" but she might as well have.

"That wasn't a special delivery for me, by any chance, was it?"

She looked me squarely in the eyes, the color rising in her sallow cheeks.

"I'm sure if it had been, Mrs. Latham, you'd have been told so at once."

"Oh, of course," I said quickly. "I didn't mean that. It's just that I have one child at school and one in the Air Force, and you always sort of hope it may be for you."

"Well, it's not," she said. She picked up her bag she'd put on the needlepoint chair against the rose-beige wall. "Now that you're here, I won't bother my aunt." She seemed in an awful hurry to get away. "Tell her I'll be back later, will you, please?"

I started to say, "Don't let me drive you away," but I didn't have a chance. She was out the door and gone. The butler, who'd come out of his pantry to answer the bell, stood smiling at the end of the hall for a moment, turned and went back again.

The special-delivery letter must have been for Elsie herself, I thought, and she'd taken it away. It wasn't on the silver tray on the table, and she'd obviously received it herself, as the squirrel had got only one walnut, and that was when the butler had opened the door for her. I don't think it would have crossed my mind, any of it, if it hadn't been for the way she'd acted—as if she'd thought I was accusing her of something, and then dashing off. And the incident was anything but closed.

I saw Abigail in the mirror on the stairs. She was half out of bed, and I know I wasn't imagining the obvious alarm that had got her that far. It was just a flash as I went by, but it was enough, and when I got to her door I was sure I hadn't been wrong. She was back in bed, as a bedridden invalid should have been, but she was sitting up as straight as a ramrod, her blue old eyes as bright as coals.

She glanced sharply at my hands. "Was that a letter, Dear Child?" Her voice was direct and sharp.

"If it was, Elsie got it," I said. "She must have just been there and taken it." I broke off sharply. "Mrs. Whitney!"

The old woman had turned the color of death. Her eyes were staring, her bony hands clutching at her throat.

"What is it?" I cried.

"Oh," she whispered. She thrust one hand out, gripping my wrist, shaking it frantically. "Go get her! Stop her! Go quickly, quickly!"

I ran out of the room and down the steps as fast as I could go, and tore open the front door. I knew it was no use, even while I was breaking my neck doing it, because I'd taken a long time getting up the stairs to give her a chance to settle herself back in bed. Elsie could have got at least a block down Walnut Street. She was nowhere in sight. She could have gone to her father's house, I thought, and I ran next door and rang the bell. It seemed to me that it took the Irish maid hours to get to the door, and when she did, she shook her head.

"Sure, and I was just this minute tellin' Miss Abby on the telephone. Miss Elsie ain't been here this morning."

I went back to the pink house and upstairs to the second floor again.

"She's gone," I said.

Abigail was just putting down the telephone. Her hands were shaking violently and she looked ghastly. I was really alarmed.

"I can't get hold of Sam," she said desperately. "None of them. Sam or Monk or Travis or my brother."

"They're probably all at the police station," I said. "Or all of them except Judge Whitney were, and I imagine they still are. Do you want me to try to get one of them for you?"

She closed her eyes and let her head fall back on her yellow cushions, shaking it back and forth.

"No, no," she whispered. "Call the Acorn Club and see if she's there. Tell her I want to speak to her. Tell her I'm dying—anything. I've got to get hold of her."

But she wasn't there, and she hadn't been in. I tried the entire roster of good works. Abigail lay there murmuring one of them after another, getting weaker and paler and bluer-gilled with each failure.

At last I said, "Now I'm going to call a doctor."

She shook her head. "There's no use," she whispered. "I'll be all right. Just go away now, Dear Child, and let me rest. Colonel Primrose wants you to meet him at eleven o'clock at the Warwick. Go now, and don't say anything about this, please. I'll take care of it my own way. Don't tell any of them, I beg you."

She held out her hand to me. When I took it, she clung to mine. "Oh, don't go. Don't leave me, Dear Child," she whispered. "I'm a wicked, terrible old woman. You must forgive me, Dear Child. . . . Oh, Douglas, Douglas!"

She still clung to me for a moment. Then abruptly she let me go, opened her eyes and sat up.

"Of course, Elsie is Very Irritating," she said with great firmness. "Now, run along, Dear Child. Your Colonel will be Waiting."

Colonel Primrose, when I met him in the comfortable and dignified lobby of the Warwick, was pacing up and down, looking from his watch to the door and back again, and pretty irritated about something.

I came up behind him. "Did you wish to see me, sir?" I asked.

He cocked his head down and around, his black eyes snapping.

"Where have you been?" he demanded. "And where in hell is Buck? I told that —— to take you to see Malone and stay with you!"

"Dear me," I said. Still, I'd often wondered if he'd managed a regiment with nothing but urbanity.

"We were otherwise engaged, both of us," I added. "And don't go military on us or we'll both quit."

"I thought you'd already quit," he retorted. "I can't do two jobs and look after you at the same time. I want you to go home and stay there. I'm——"

"Colonel Primrose," a voice said. "Paging Colonel Primrose."

He broke off and diverted a lethal glare to the bellboy.

"Here," he snapped.

"Gentleman at the desk to see you, sir. Shall I send him over? Gentleman with the straw hat, sir."

Colonel Primrose looked, and nodded curtly.

I saw that the gentleman with the straw hat was Pete Martin, of *The Saturday Evening Post.* His big camel's-hair coat was hanging open down to his ankles, the belt not tied. The straw hat was a Panama that had seen many better winters. It was battered, shapeless, and aged a variegated ginger brown. Surrounded as he was by women wrapped in mink and men in heavy overcoats and scarves who kept glancing at him and edging away a little, he was doing an embarrassed best to pretend he had just picked it up on the way in. He came over, sort of bumbling and red-faced.

"I wonder if I could talk to you, colonel. I've just been——" He saw me and stopped. "Oh, I beg your pardon." He fumbled with the straw hat and got a shade redder. "It was on the hook," he said. "I guess I just grabbed it without noticing. I——"

Colonel Primrose waited stiffly. That he was still mad at me and Buck, Pete Martin had no way of knowing. The big editor grew a little redder-faced, fumbled in his overcoat pocket for his handkerchief, pulled it out and mopped his forehead. He put the handkerchief back in his pocket, or thought he did. It got between his coat and belt and fell, unnoticed by him, onto the carpet. I started to say something, and stopped, not entirely of my own volition. Colonel Primrose's steely glance rested on me for a bare instant, and I knew he'd seen it too.

Lying quite open-faced on the rug, almost as if chance had deliberately arranged it that way, was the monogram Captain Malone had smoothed out on his desk. Or its mate, rather, done in shaded blue instead of shaded tan. The T wasn't upside down and the middle letter wasn't a W, it was an M. It read "$W\,T\,M$," not "$M\,T\,W$." It wasn't for Monckton Tyler Whitney. It was for W. Thornton Martin.

I stood dumbly, trying not to look at it lying there beside

118

his foot, hearing those voices through the iron grille vent in the washroom on *The Saturday Evening Post* sixth floor, saying, "Where the hell was Pete? . . . Pipe down about Pete. . . ."

More immediately I could hear Colonel Primrose saying, "I'm busy right now. Unless it's urgent. I can see you at the *Post* this afternoon."

Of course it was urgent. People don't dash out in an aged straw hat in the middle of January unless something's on their mind they've got to get off.

"I don't guess it's very urgent," Pete Martin said. He was rather like a large friendly sheepdog, abashed at making an error he didn't quite know the nature of. He backed off with a grin.

Colonel Primrose reached down and picked up his handkerchief.

"Then it wasn't Monk's handkerchief," I said.

"As Malone knows perfectly well," he said. "If you people would quit jumping to the first conclusion you see, it would simplify matters considerably. You've let Malone tie you all up in bowknots. If you'd acted like normal, intelligent human beings——" He shrugged.

"Has he put Monk in jail yet?" I inquired sweetly.

"I expect one of you will manage it before noon. You've got forty-five minutes yet."

He took a deep breath, counting ten, no doubt.

"Damn it," he said. "If I could only get hold of that manuscript."

"Perhaps I could help you if you'd be at all civil," I said calmly. "Civil instead of military."

He didn't snap this time. He looked at me earnestly for a moment. "That is what I was afraid of," he said soberly. "That's why I wanted Buck not to let you out of his sight."

I drew a blank at that one.

"You know, sometimes, Mrs. Latham," he said, "I think you ought to have your I. Q. determined. Or maybe it's better never to know." He looked at his watch. "I've got a sitting room on the third floor. Come along. I want to talk to you."

"I hope Sergeant Buck won't mind," I said, when we got out of the elevator.

"Sergeant Buck won't mind anything when I'm through with him," he said grimly. He opened the door.

It was a pleasant room with an electric icebox humming away in a small kitchen off the foyer.

"Sit down," he said. "Don't you realize a man has been murdered in cold blood, right in sight of God knows how many persons, on account of that manuscript? And here you go wandering around in the middle of the night as if the world was a field of buttercups. Who knows you've got that manuscript?"

"You and I," I said.

"Are you sure?"

"I think so. At least, unless Myron told somebody else, which I doubt."

He thought for a moment and nodded. "Go ahead," he said shortly.

"Well, there's nothing to go ahead with, really," I retorted. I was getting a little mad myself. "Myron told me he'd sent a copy of his script to my house in care of me. Somebody was prying into his papers, and he wanted a copy in reserve, I suppose."

I hesitated. I didn't know quite how much to tell him, and then I decided that, since Abigail had got the document back, it didn't matter, really.

"I thought first he'd sent what they all call a document he got by mistake from Judge Whitney's files down, too, but he said he hadn't," I went on. "And they've got it back anyway."

He was looking at me with a kind of pained incredulity that I found a little irritating.

"Don't be absurd," I said. "He had to send it somewhere—the script—and he said my address was the only one in Washington he could remember offhand. There's no reason why he shouldn't have."

He shook his head silently, went to the sofa, sat down and picked up the telephone on the table at the end of it.

"Get me Washington, Hobart One-five-nine-six," he said.

"What are you doing?"

It was my phone number in Georgetown.

"I'm having that manuscript sent to Captain Malone," he said calmly. "Then you're going to Judge Whitney's with me for lunch, and you're going to tell them you've done it. You're going to tell your friend Abigail. I'm going to call Ben Hibbs and tell him. We'll have a notice put on the front page of—what is the paper in Philadelphia everybody's supposed to read? For the simple reason that I don't want you to have a knife between your ribs. God knows why, but I don't. It's——" He turned back to the telephone. "Hello. . . . Yes. Hello. . . . Lilac?"

Lilac is my colored cook, and the angel without whom for twenty years, life would never have been so gay, or stormy at times, but always fundamentally secure in the honesty and dependability and affection of the best friend I've ever had.

"This is Colonel Primrose. . . . Yes, she's here. She's fine. I'm fine. . . . Yes, it's very cold here."

You can't ever talk long distance to Lilac without an intimate discussion of the weather.

"Now listen to me, Lilac. A friend of Miss Grace's sent some mail in care—— What's that?" He listened for a long time, his face settling into soberer and soberer lines.

My I. Q. may be too low to risk the public shame of having it measured, but I knew what she was saying. I knew it before he said, "All right. Here she is. You can talk to her."

He handed me the phone.

"Hello, Lilac," I said. . . . "Yes, I'm very well. . . . No, it isn't snowing here. What's this about Mr. Kane's mail?"

"Mr. Kane he called up yes'dy an' said I was to send it to him in Philadelphia, at the address you was stayin' at, an' did I have it, an' I said 'deed I did. He says I was to send it special delivery right away. Now what does he mean sayin' he ain'?"

"What time did he call, Lilac?" I asked.

"It was half pas' three. He say it was important, and would I get myself a taxi and go to the main post office and ask th' man where was the box to put it in, so it would go right away. He say he would give me the money for the taxi when he come down next time."

"Thanks, Lilac," I said. We talked about a lot of other things before I could ring off. At last I put the phone down.

"Myron Kane called her at half past three," I said.

Myron had been dead for some time just then, and neither of us bothered to say it.

I said instead, "Elsie Phelps has that script now, colonel. Judge Whitney's married daughter, Sam Phelps' wife."

He waited for me to go on, and I did. I told him about the

121

taxi driver, and the squirrel, and the special-delivery letter
Elsie said wasn't for me. And about Abigail Whitney sending
me dashing after her, and the scene I'd had with her, calling
up all over town, trying to get hold of Elsie. The only thing
I didn't tell him was about her crying "Douglas, Douglas" as
she clung to my hand. I couldn't tell him that without telling
him about Judge Whitney and Douglas Elliot, Travis' father,
and that whole story of embezzlement and murder.

He listened to me silently. When I was through, he got up
and walked over to the window. He stood looking down on
the Locust Street crowds hurrying back and forth. He came
back to the sofa and picked up the phone.

"Lombard Six-five hundred," he said.

"Who are you calling?" I asked.

"Ben Hibbs. I want them to know Elsie Phelps has the
script. Or I don't really. All I really want them to know is
you haven't it."

I looked at him blankly. "I thought you thought none of
them——"

"Mr. Ben Hibbs, please. . . . Hello, Ben, this is John Primrose. Elsie Phelps—you remember her, Whitney's daughter—
has a copy of Myron's profile of the judge, if you still want
to run it. . . . Yes, I'm going to see her—this afternoon if I
can. . . . Right. I'll try to get it for you. You might let the
boys know, by the way. And tell Pete I'm sorry I was short
with him. I'll see him later. Good-by."

He put down the phone and stood with his hand resting on
it for a few minutes, looking fixedly past and beyond it.
Then he turned to me and smiled, shaking his head slowly.

"I'm sorry," he said. "The thing we've got to do now is get
hold of Elsie Phelps."

It was five minutes past twelve then. Elsie wasn't at home.
The maid said she wouldn't be home until half past five. At
half past four they found her. She was lying face down on
the frozen bank of Wissahickon Creek, out toward German-
town. The reason they hadn't found her before was that
there was a clump of laurel bushes between her and the
driveway.

She had been there since half past twelve, the police said.
Her watch had struck a stone when she fell.

Tossed in the bushes, they found a heavy bronze medallion. It had Benjamin Franklin's profile in relief on the face,

122

and on the reverse side an engraved picture of The Curtis Publishing Company Building:

COMMEMORATING THE
200TH ANNIVERSARY
"THE SATURDAY
EVENING POST"
1728   FOUNDED BY   1928
BENJAMIN FRANKLIN

The people at the *Post* all had them on their desks for paper weights.

The one they found in the laurel bushes had blood on it, and there was a sharp, deep cut on Elsie Phelps' head where the bronze rim of the medallion had struck her.

13

But when we were lunching with Judge Nathaniel Whitney at a quarter past one, we naturally didn't know that Elsie Phelps was dead, and I may say the conversation would have been very different if we had. If we had, that is, and there'd still been a lunch.

We were supposed to be at the house at one o'clock, but after I'd told Colonel Primrose about Elsie and the special-delivery letter, and about the scene Abigail had put on, I was too involved to stop. Or rather, I suppose, I'd given Colonel Primrose a lever to pry the rest of it out with. I can see now that I was put through a third degree—the rubber-hose-in-the-velvet-stocking sort of thing—and it's a wonder to me that I managed to hold out as much as I did. The handkerchief with W. Thornton Martin's monogram on it, not Monckton Tyler Whitney's, lying on the table in front of me, was no doubt put there on purpose, as a reminder that if it was Monk I was worried about, I didn't have to be any longer. It was a childish ruse, but Colonel Primrose had already said I was simple-minded, and I guess I am.

I told him why I'd come, in the first place, and about that document that Laurel had given Myron by mistake, and about Mr. Toplady's letter, and about Mr. Toplady generally, but not about the conversation I'd had with him on the bench in the square. Nor did I tell him about Abigail and Judge Whitney, nor about what Monk had told me the night before, about Travis' father using Laurel's money and supposedly committing suicide. I thought, in fact, I really did a very good job of keeping faith with Monk, as I'd promised I would do.

And then I discovered it wasn't interest in what I was telling him that was keeping us there when we were supposed to be at Judge Whitney's at one. It was because Sergeant Buck hadn't come. When he did come, Colonel Primrose took him into the bedroom and closed the door. He came out a little later and we left immediately. He must have unburdened himself, I thought, because he was in a vastly better humor. It was too bad that I hadn't had courage to listen at the keyhole.

Our being late didn't matter, however, because Monk and Travis were just going in as we got to that side of the square, and Laurel had taken us upstairs to the back library before Judge Whitney himself came in.

They all looked pretty grim, frankly. The judge covered it up fairly well, and so did Laurel and Travis. Monk didn't even try to. He wasn't sullen exactly, but he sat with us but not of us, and if you'd taken his face without any of the background, you might have thought he sensed a polecat in the room, although Sam hadn't come yet. It wasn't Laurel, either, because neither of them seemed even to see the other. She was spared having to offer him a glass of sherry when he got up, went to the cellarette and poured himself a bourbon and water, emphasizing his nonconformity to the household mores.

Judge Whitney looked at his watch. "Where are Sam and Elsie?" he asked. . . . "I wanted you to meet all the members of the family, Colonel Primrose."

"Soapy had a busy day ahead of him," Monk said.

"Does he know, I wonder," Colonel Primrose asked blandly, "that his wife is in possession of what seems to be a very dangerous document?"

Laurel, who'd taken a chair where her back was all Monk could have seen of her if he had cared to look, which he didn't, glanced quickly at me. She was taut and tense again, the way she'd been the first day, when the responsibility for the document Myron had was still entirely hers. She looked away as quickly.

I realized that Colonel Primrose was only trying to find out if they knew about it, and there was no doubt they all did. There was a well of silence, not long, but fathoms deep.

"Aunt Abby told him, sir," Travis said at last. "She called the police station. That's why he left without waiting to see Malone. I don't get it, because he said Kane showed him the manuscript, and there was nothing in it anybody could object to. But he sure got out of there in a hurry. Boy, did he go!"

125

"He didn't say where he was going, Mr. Travis?"

Travis hesitated for just an instant. I think he was going to correct Colonel Primrose about his name, but it would have been rather awkward, and he let it go.

"No, sir," he said.

Judge Whitney looked at his watch again. He nodded to the maid who'd come to the door. "We won't wait for them any longer."

"Elsie is probably at a Meeting," Travis said.

We went downstairs to the large dining room across the back of the house. It was dark and heavy, with beautiful gleaming silver on an oak sideboard and closets full of lovely old china and porcelain along one whole side of the room. Whatever sun there was wasn't enough to get very far, and the overhead lights didn't help out too much.

Judge Whitney had me at his right and Colonel Primrose at his left. The two Phelpses' seats yawned empty beside us, and then came Monk on my side, Laurel at the end and Travis next to her.

"Of course, Colonel Primrose, it's a very curious thing to me," Judge Whitney said. "I've no idea why my family is so determined that this profile of mine has to be censored or why it's regarded as dangerous. It's a complete and total mystery to me."

"You didn't see it, I understand?"

"No," Judge Whitney said deliberately. "I didn't want to."

He avoided looking at the three members of his family—actual or virtual—at the end of the table, where they were sitting like children with their eyes on their plates.

"Once in a city out West—Tacoma, Washington, I think it was—I was walking through a public park," he went on quietly. "I've forgotten now whether it was a bust of Ibsen or a full figure I came on. But there was a tablet on it with a quotation from him that I've never forgotten. It said:

"Our lives should be pure and white
Tablets whereon God may write.

"I'm not so presumptuous as to pretend that I've followed that edict to the letter, but I think I can say there's nothing in my life I would object to having published in *The Saturday Evening Post*."

Monk was the only one of the three who wasn't looking at

him then. A dull flush had deepened the color in his sun-burned face. His eyes were still fixed on his plate.

"I've made mistakes," Judge Whitney said calmly. "A great many of them. I've done as many small and petty things I'm ashamed of as any man, and I wouldn't flaunt them in public. But I have an idea that if Myron Kane had stumbled on any of them, it might be good for my soul to have them exposed."

He turned his fine white head and strong blue eyes toward Colonel Primrose, smiling faintly.

"I think a profile ought to include a glimpse of the clay everyone's feet are made of. That's why I like the modern profile method. It's an insult to every man's intelligence to pretend, as the old biographies did, that the subject was flawless. That's what makes for our common humanity." He glanced at the three at the end of the table again and smiled. "For one thing, I understand Myron Kane made it very clear he thought I had, in a sense, adopted Laurel Frazier and concerned myself professionally with other people's children, because I'd done such an unsatisfactory job with my own."

His smile as his eyes rested with great pride on Monk was a palpable denial. Monk's eyes were still on his plate, and the ears and mind he was listening with were too beclouded to catch the gentle raillery in his father's tone. His jaw tightened and the flush on his face darkened.

"I'm sorry, sir," he said. His own tone was clipped and curt. "You won't have to put up with me after tomorrow. My leave's up and I'll be glad to steer clear of Philadelphia hereafter. And as Elsie's apt to get her throat cut any time now, you'll be rid of her too. I'll be glad to do it myself, if it'll help you out any."

His father had raised his glass of sauterne. He held it halfway to his lips, completely stunned, looking blankly across the table.

"Oh, Monk!" Laurel said. "You ought to——"

"You can shut up, please," Monk said quietly. "Furthermore, I hope somebody's told you the handkerchief you tried to palm off on Malone wasn't mine, after all. You didn't burn the right corner. What——"

Travis Elliot put his wineglass down. "Come on, Monk. Cut it out."

Laurel was sitting bolt upright, her lips parted. "It—it wasn't yours?" she whispered.

"No, Sweetie-pie." He spoke with elaborate irony. "It wasn't mine, and you knew damned well it wasn't."

Colonel Primrose's urbane glance moved from one to the other of them. Judge Whitney sat there silently. The whole activity of the table centered in the young maelstrom swirling up at the other end.

Travis pushed his chair back a little, his jaw beginning to stick out too. "Monk," he said quietly, "you don't know what you're saying." He had a good deal of force under his well-tailored exterior. "Just shut up, will you?"

Laurel flashed around, the color suddenly flaming up like two geranium petals in her cheeks. "Will you be quiet yourself, Travis?"

Judge Whitney's hand came down on the table sharply. "That makes it unanimous," he said. "I suggest all three of you shut up. I don't understand this—any of it. I don't understand you—any of you. I'm astonished that you—— Colonel Primrose, Mrs. Latham, I hope——"

If Mr. Samuel Phelps had tried to plan his entrance for the worst possible moment, he couldn't have done it better. He came bravely in through the living-room door, his bald head pink and glistening, rubbing his hands together.

"I'm very sorry I'm late, sir," he said.

The atmosphere was crackling with static. Judge Whitney fixed his blue eyes on him. "Where is my daughter?"

Sam Phelps stopped in his tracks, looking at the two empty chairs. I glanced at Colonel Primrose. He was still looking quietly around. Laurel had picked up her Waterford goblet, the bright pink stain still visible in her cheeks. The pulse in her throat was going a mile a minute. Monk and Travis were both staring grimly down at the table.

"I thought she would be here, sir." Sam spoke politely, if not very tranquilly, and he was obviously not happy. "May I sit down, sir? I don't care for anything to eat." He sat down between Colonel Primrose and Travis.

"I assume you're aware, Sam, of what Elsie has done," Judge Whitney said quietly.

"I think we can trust her discretion, sir." There was something very smug about the way he said it.

"I'm afraid I don't quite understand you."

I don't know why Sam missed the storm warnings. They were certainly plain.

"I mean you don't have to disturb yourself about the—the document any more, Judge Whitney."

It wasn't only smug then, it was slightly patronizing. I didn't dare look at anyone.

"I mean, I'm sure Elsie will destroy it at once."

I looked at Travis then. He'd put his hand out to Laurel and was holding hers tightly on the edge of the table. She'd gone the color of the meringue under the fresh strawberries on her plate, the blue of her eyes drained until they were gray.

"If you'll pardon me, sir," Travis said abruptly, "I think Sam had better explain what he and Aunt Abby have been doing. I think you should listen, sir."

Judge Whitney looked at him silently, and glanced at Monk, still sitting there like a hundred-and-ninety-pound Hamlet in contemporary dress, absorbed in a wordless soliloquy. He looked at Laurel and at Travis, and nodded.

"What have you and my sister been doing, Sam?" he asked.

"I would rather tell you in private, sir." Sam's collar seemed higher and tighter. He glanced sideways at Colonel Primrose.

"I prefer to hear it now," Judge Whitney said.

"Very well, sir. It's merely that Aunt Abby learned this fellow Kane had sent the document he got from Laurel—she says by mistake—down to Mrs. Latham's house in Washington. I lunched with Aunt Abby yesterday, at her request. She suggested I telephone Mrs. Latham's house and have Kane's mail sent back here. We know it was the only way to get the —the document in the proper hands again."

The silence then was deep and long as well.

"You see, that was before we knew Kane was dead," Sam said. "It was . . . unfortunate, of course," he added lamely.

Still nobody spoke.

"I was acting in what I regarded as the family's best interest."

He waited, and was starting to add something when Judge Whitney interrupted him. "Thank you, Sam," he said.

If you have seen a soft crab dropped into a kettle of smoking fat, you will know what Sam Phelps looked like just then. I wouldn't have believed three words could so wither and burn. It was fortunate the maid came in then.

"The telephone, sir," she said.

Laurel jumped up. "I'll answer it, sir."

The silence continued a moment after she'd got out. To

129

my surprise, it was Colonel Primrose who broke it; and after a moment I was more than surprised.

"I ran across some curious ancient history this morning," he said—"While Miss Frazier is gone. I was at the Quaker Trust Company, having some microfilm records run off on the screen. The bookkeeper—his name is Toplady—got an extra roll in by mistake. They were films of the famous Douglas Elliot steal of ten years ago, and the note you'd signed the day he blew his brains——"

If a bolt of lightning had struck the table, we couldn't, any of us, have been more appalled or more rigidly speechless with horror. Colonel Primrose stopped abruptly, sensing it, as he would, but still, of course, not realizing.

"I—I'm sorry!" he said. He looked quickly at the door. "I was sure she was out of hearing. I'm very sorry!"

I have never seen people more aghast—even Sam—and all of us trying to look anywhere but at Travis.

Monk pushed his chair back. "Excuse me, please, father," he said shortly. He got up. . . . "Come on, Trav."

Travis got up slowly. "My name is Travis Elliot, Colonel Primrose," he said quietly. "Douglas Elliot was my father. Will you excuse me, please, sir?"

Judge Whitney came around the table and put his hand on Travis' shoulder. "If you'll wait, son, I think Colonel Primrose would like the privilege of being allowed to tell you he didn't——"

If it hadn't all been so awful, the sight of Colonel Primrose's face would have been irresistibly funny.

Travis shook his head. "It doesn't matter, sir. It was a steal, and my father did blow his brains out. I—I can't ask—— Just excuse me, sir. Will you, please?"

Monk was waiting for him in the door. He was looking back at his father. He didn't speak, but just looked at him. They went on out.

Colonel Primrose had got himself together and got to his feet, knocking over his wineglass as he did it.

"I'm very sorry, Judge Whitney," he said quietly. "I—I understood the young man's name to be Travis. I—you know, I wouldn't for the world have——"

"I know, indeed, you would not have," Judge Whitney said. He let himself down heavily in his chair and sat there, looking down at the table. "It can't be helped, colonel. Travis has had a good deal to forgive a good many people—including his father before and at his death. I—I didn't know

130

the records were still in existence. It was a very great trag-edy." He got slowly up. "I think, if you will excuse me now —— I don't wish to be rude, but I—I feel the need of a little rest."

We went out of the dining room. All of us, that is, but Sam Phelps. At the door, I glanced back. Nobody else seemed to notice that he was still sitting at the table.

14

"I don't want to rub it in, but if you just hadn't been so brutal about it——" I said as we left the house. "Did you have to call it a steal? And couldn't you have said something besides 'blew his brains out'?"

He gave me a rueful glance. "I'm sorry," he said briefly.

We were walking toward Walnut Street in silence after that, because it seemed to me that it was hardly sufficient apology for such an incredibly inept breach of courtesy.

"I guess it must have been that Ibsen quotation," he said as we reached the corner. He repeated the lines Judge Whitney had spoken:

> *"Our lives should be pure and white*
> *Tablets whereon God may write."*

He was silent a moment.

"You see, I knew Douglas Elliot," he said. "He was in the Judge Advocate General's Department in the last war. I never knew a man whose life was a whiter tablet for God to write on. It made me very sore. Stupid, I suppose, but there it is."

I didn't know what he meant, but I thought I had a fairly good idea. He always knew things I never gave him credit for knowing, and if he knew what Monk and I knew, that quotation, coming from Judge Whitney, must have sounded like the crassest and most hypocritical bombast and deceit. I knew that was what it had sounded like, and sickeningly, to Monk. It hadn't to me, but I'm easily affected by what I believe is called theater. And it was good theater, at that. Still, to anyone inclined to be a realist or with a personal connection I didn't have, I could see how it would have sounded, knowing the tablet of the judge's life was splotched with the blood of his friend.

132

Anyway, I decided I'd better go back and tell Monk it wasn't I who'd told Colonel Primrose—or not so far as I knew.

"I'll go back to Abigail's, I think," I said.

He smiled faintly. "You're going with me."

He hailed a taxi.

"To the Warwick, please. After that I want to go to Camden."

"You mean New Jersey?" I demanded. My knowledge of geography being pre-Copernican, I had no way of knowing it was just across the river and not as far as Capitol Hill is from my house in Georgetown.

It seemed to me an embarrassingly long time that he was in the Warwick, but that was, no doubt, because so many people wanted the taxi in which I was parked outside.

He came out at last and said to the driver, "Three hundred ten Pepperell Street."

"Who lives on Pepperell Street?" I asked.

"Albert Toplady."

I said, "Oh."

He cocked his head down and around again, and looked at me this time, sharply.

"Will he be home?" I asked.

"Yes. He will."

No. 310 was painted bright yellow, with white trim, and it had a whitewashed picket fence around its minute lot, with a star-shaped flower bed marked with whitewashed bricks as a front garden. The shades were drawn in the two front windows and there was a bottle of milk on the porch.

"Well, it doesn't look as if anybody's at home," I said.

We went up to the door. I noticed two women peering out at us through the orange curtain of the window next door. They were still there when Colonel Primrose gave up ringing the doorbell after several minutes.

"I'll go around to the back," he said. "You wait here."

I waited. I could hear him banging on the back door, but either Mr. Toplady was not at home or Mr. Toplady had no intention of coming out. The taxi driver got back into his car and settled down. Colonel Primrose came back.

One of the watching women came out on her front porch. "He's home, all right," she said. "I saw him go in." She looked at me and back at Colonel Primrose. "Are you and your daughter relations of his?"

"Just friends," Colonel Primrose said, only slightly discomfited.

"A lot of people been coming here to see him the last few days," the woman said. "My goodness, I've never seen the like of it before. A gentleman came last night—he had white hair—and just before him a young, red-haired lady came."

"Is that so?" Colonel Primrose said politely.

"And there was another man. And now you two. He's never had any visitors before, in all the time we've lived here."

Colonel Primrose murured something. His face was puzzled and very grave. "I don't understand this," he said. "I'm damned if I——"

He banged on the door again, and waited. There was no sound inside the little house. Then he got down suddenly on one knee, cupped his hands around the keyhole and peered in. He gave a sudden startled exclamation, got up, took a step back and lunged into the door with all his weight. The cheap frame splintered and the lock snapped like brittle taffy. He went on quickly into the room and stopped short.

In the instant before he said, "Get back, Mrs. Latham," I saw what he had seen. It was Albert Toplady. He had a blue automatic in his hand, and his hand was raised. His face was gray and terrible as he stared at us, his hand shaking so that the gun was aimed God knows where. All I know is that I saw the muzzle of it, and it was aimed Colonel Primrose's way then. And—well, I've always underestimated him, I guess. He walked deliberately across the room toward Mr. Toplady, the little man backing off into the corner, his finger trembling on the trigger of the gun.

And I heard Colonel Primrose saying quietly, "I'll take that, Mr. Toplady. It might go off."

He went up to him and took the pistol out of his hand, and then, as Albert Toplady suddenly collapsed, he caught him, moved a chair with one foot and let him gently down into it. I came on in, rather more than half paralyzed. That's when I became aware of the room itself, and I was so dumfounded that I didn't hear Colonel Primrose tell me to close the door until he came back and did it himself. He put up the window shades then, and I could see everything clearly in that unbelievable room.

It was a shrine to Myron Kane. There wasn't a foot of wall space that didn't have his picture on it. They were all framed, and there were framed newspaper clippings. Some of the pictures had been cut from newspapers, others photographed from newspapers and book originals. Some of them were so enlarged that they were gray and indistinct. On a table against the wall was a large, thick, green-covered scrap-book. It lay there like the family Bible, and printed on it was WRITINGS OF MYRON KANE, THE GREAT CORRESPONDENT. And more. Lying across the table by the scrapbook, beside copies of the three books he'd written, was Myron Kane's ebony walking stick with the silver presentation plaque on the crook handle.

Mr. Toplady, gray and shaking, stared down at the floor, his hands moving aimlessly. I looked blankly at Colonel Primrose. He was standing there, his eyes moving slowly over the rows on rows of the handsome face on all the walls. He looked down then at the little man.

"He was your son?" He asked it as gently as if he were speaking to a sick child.

A convulsive tremor shook Albert Toplady's body. "I never told anybody," he said. "He thought I did. But I wouldn't disgrace him. I've never said anything, not to any-body."

It was so horribly clear, then—Myron's collapse when he didn't get the letter I'd brought for him, and he thought the Whitneys would know. *The snob, the beastly snob,* I thought, and I tried to avoid the confident arrogance of the face plastered on the flimsy walls of the pathetic jerry-built little house.

Mr. Toplady sensed what we were thinking, for Colonel Primrose must have been thinking it too. He looked up with a kind of pitiful appeal.

"It wasn't his fault. It was our fault. He couldn't sign himself Albert Toplady—people would laugh. Myron Kane was his mother's grandfather's name. He was like him, big and handsome. He took it at school because the boys made fun of his name. We sent him to private schools, so he'd make influential friends. We wanted him to know important people and get ahead in the world, not be kept down to our level. We didn't realize, until it was too late——"

He put his head down on the table, one hand resting on Myron's stick, his shoulders racked and shaking, sobbing without making a sound. It came to me suddenly, and not unkindly, that he had got what he wanted, in a way, because the silver plate on that stick bore the donor's name, and it was a very important name indeed.

Colonel Primrose was talking to him as I went out. I had to leave. I couldn't take it any longer. Not when everywhere I turned I had to look at Myron while I had another picture of him in my own mind—the morning he came back to

Abigail's, unshaven and bitter against the Whitneys and the world. I knew now where he'd been; he didn't have his stick then, and he had had it the night before when he'd slipped on the ice in front of Travis' door. He was still saying, then, that he'd be ruined. It wasn't his father so much, then, as the front he'd built up, in the Press Who's Who that Colonel Primrose had once quoted from, and his perjured passport, and those sketches of his life on the dust covers of his books. It would be ridicule that would ruin him, if it ever got out.

I walked out to the picket fence and stood there a little while. I'd started to go back in when I heard the telephone ringing inside, and I stopped as I heard Colonel Primrose.

His voice was grave and urgent. ". . . he would call. If it is him, Mr. Toplady, tell him what I told you, and tell him you're leaving here at once. Your life depends on it."

I went back, quietly and quickly. I had a sudden overpowering desire not to be even within telephone earshot of a voice I might be able to recognize. It seemed to me that what Myron Kane had got had been definitely coming to him. He was too intelligent and too able a man to have let himself live in a glasshouse that any chance stone could bring shattering down around his head. I looked back at the little house. Myron's income had been enormous from his syndicated stuff and magazine articles and radio and books. He could at least have repaid what had been spent on him at the fancy schools or he could at least have sent one picture autographed with the flourish that was on the quite unsolicited one that I had in a drawer at home.

As I went out the gate to get into the taxi, the door of a house across the street opened and Sergeant Buck came out. I wouldn't have been surprised if it had been Daniel Boone or the Duke of Wellington. I'd reached the point of saturation. Sergeant Buck spat at some microcosmic detail in the middle of the street and I'm sure hit it on the nose, came on over and went in through Mr. Toplady's gate, brother to the insensate rock, and only irritating to me when I suddenly thought how easy it would have been for Mr. Toplady's aspen-leaf fingers to have sent Colonel Primrose permanently to Arlington.

Colonel Primrose came out and got into the taxi.

"Don't ever do that again," I said.

He stared at me. "Don't do what?" Then he said, "Oh." He shook his head soberly. "He'd have blown his brains out if I hadn't. . . . Curtis Building, driver, and as quickly as you can, please."

He looked back, and I did too. Sergeant Buck was stationed out on Mr. Toplady's porch. It's the nearest I've ever come to seeing a man literally as big as a house.

"How did you know about Myron?" I asked as we turned out of Pepperell Street.

"You practically told me," he said. "You know, I've always thought there was something phony about Myron. With that Who's Who record, he just couldn't have been such a damned snob. The idea occurred to me when you told me about Toplady, and the awe in his voice when he said Mr. Kane was right there in the same house with Mrs. Whitney. The odds were heavy on something personal in that. Of course, when I first saw all those pictures——" He stared ahead very gravely for a moment. Then he looked at me and smiled. "That isn't why I came out. You're making the same mistake Myron made. We've got a picture here with murder in it, Mrs. Latham, and nobody in the picture gives a damn who Myron's father is. Incidentally, if they'd brought him up at a public school and taught him, at home, to respect decent and honest people, he'd have gone a lot farther than he did, because at the age of forty-two he'd still be alive."

"What do you mean?" I demanded.

"If Myron had been—well, let's say a better man, he wouldn't have taken advantage of a situation he found himself in, to do harm to another person. Thereby goading said other person into sticking a knife into him. That's all I mean. Myron believed in living, but not letting live, and it backfired. And now, Mrs. Latham, be quiet. I really need to think this time. We're meeting Malone at Curtis'."

But I couldn't be quiet at that point, even though I saw clearly that not doing so meant a complete reversal of my own position when I'd fled from the front porch to the taxi. This sounded too much like Abigail's speech, via me, to Laurel, about destroying a useful life. Myron wasn't the only one who believed in living but not letting live.

"Are you holding a brief for murder?" I demanded.

He looked around at me with annoyance at first, and then sharp intentness. "Not at all. I expect to get Myron's murderer before—— But that's not what you mean?"

I caught myself just in time. If I could only learn to be quiet when I was told to be, I thought.

"He's the only person who's been murdered, isn't he?" I said.

He looked at me very oddly for an instant. Then he looked at his watch. "It's twenty-five minutes past three," he said. "Malone's meeting me at the *Post* as soon as we can get there. Now, if you think you can keep still for about five minutes—— I don't want to tax you unduly, of course."

The man who had seen Franklin was at the desk in the marble lobby. He told us to go on up, that Captain Malone was on the sixth floor, waiting. Captain Malone was on the sixth floor, but he wasn't waiting. He appeared to be going right ahead. He'd taken over Day Edgar's cubbyhole on the Walnut Street side and was looking down at that moment, very sardonically, at a pile of reports in front of him. He nodded to Colonel Primrose and gave me an odd glance, but he even pushed a chair up for me after he'd closed the door.

"I've had the boys getting a line on all these people," he said. He shuffled through the papers on the desk. "Here. Take a copy of the *Post* and turn to the masthead in back."

He pushed a copy of the magazine over to each of us.

"There's a sign over in the promotion department that says 'You don't have to be crazy to work here, but it helps.' I suggested they move it over here. They had a cold-blooded murder in the lobby here a day ago, and this is the sort of thing they do after hours, as of last night. These are the ones that haven't got an alibi they can prove backwards and forwards. They sure lead a blameless and uneventful life." He looked at the masthead. "Benjamin Franklin's first. No alibi. He parked his clothes in Mr. Nelson's filing cabinet and disappeared."

He gave us a dour smile.

"I'm skipping all those can prove alibis. E. N. Brandt. He left early and went over to the Franklin Institute and shepherded eleven kids through the place. He went home, ate dinner and went down in the cellar to rig up a periscope so a guy flat on his back could read in bed. That was for the next one, Stuart Rose. He's in the hospital. Mr. Brandt was all right about being tailed, but he got a little sore when he found out one of his kids had showed my man his boxful of decorations from the last war. . . .

"W. T. Martin. We'll take him later."

He laid one of the reports aside.

"Jack Alexander. No alibi. We thought we had something on him. He left here and met a beautiful blonde. They went to an Italian restaurant and then headed for Delancey Place. But it turns out the beautiful blonde is his wife and they went to Delancey Place because there's a house there they're thinking of buying."

Captain Malone shook his head.

138

"Frederic Nelson. Some damn fool over at the second division had him try on the clothes in his filing cabinet. The coat would have been enough, almost. He headed for the Main Line last night, took his two English refugees to a movie and left his daughter at a school party, aired the cocker spaniel and spent the rest of the evening trying to fix the hot-water tank until my man felt sorry for him and fixed it. I might as well run a plumber's shop."

He took another report.

"Arthur Baum. He went out and ate supper and came back here. That looked interesting, but he went to his office, read a manuscript for a little while and then went out to that long sofa out there and went to sleep. He woke up at nine-thirty and went to a hotel and went to bed. Seems he likes to stay in town, so as he can work nights, because he lives on a farm up in Bucks County.

"Next is Harley Cook. He's got one of my best men in the hospital with bronchial pneumonia. He snakes out of here without an overcoat, so my man follows with just his hat on. They start out walking, and my God, they end up ten miles out in the country. How in the hell's—pardon me, Mrs. Latham—my man to know Mr. Cook's just taking his evening stroll? It's twenty-eight degrees, and by the time my man gets back, he's out like a light. Mr. Cook does some homework, and bless me if he doesn't walk back in here this morning, and still no overcoat." He looked grimly down at the report.

"I take it," Colonel Primrose said blandly, "that you're closing in on Pete Martin?"

Captain Malone looked at him. "The defense," he said imperturbably, "to be temporarily unsound of mind. Do you know what he did last night? He beat it straight from the office to the train and went to Chester. Do you know what he did in Chester? He went to a roller-skating rink. Well, if he likes to roller-skate and talk to those half-pint Jezebels that hang around roller-skating rinks, I guess that's his business." He shuffled through his papers and took one out. "This," he said, "is more like my business. Round ten o'clock on the day Kane was murdered, he went to Joe Moscowitz's and hired the Benjamin Franklin outfit. He waited while Joe let out the belt and shoulder seams. He got the wig there too. He came back through the Seventh and Sansom Street entrance on the other side and took the elevator up to the ninth floor. That was around a quarter to twelve. He stopped and talked to Andrew Hesington—that's the boy whose knife did the job. Hesington was just knocking off to go to lunch, and he remembers now that Martin didn't seem to be in any hurry. Well, Mr. Martin had to go through the composing room to get over to this side. The boy on the elevator remembers bringing him down to the sixth floor with a bundle under his arm. He asked if the *Post* crowd had gone to lunch yet, and the boy told him he'd just taken a bunch of them down. He got off at the sixth floor and went into the washroom. He left a half dozen fingerprints on the woodwork. They look like graphite smudges, but they come out clear enough to make me believe in Santa Claus again. He washed up, apparently, and then he went to his office. His secretary saw him when she came in from lunch at one o'clock. He gave her some work, and nobody remembers seeing him again until considerably after Kane's body was found. Except——"

He looked across the desk at Colonel Primrose.

"This afternoon, when Miss Frazier learned that the initials on the handkerchief she tried to burn weren't *MTW*, but *W T M*, she admitted to me she found it in a phone booth on the second floor."

"May one inquire what Miss Frazier was doing in a phone booth on the second floor?" Colonel Primrose asked.

Captain Malone nodded. "She's anxious the judge doesn't know, and I promised her I wouldn't tell him. She's decided to quit her job as his secretary, and came down here to apply for one. She came in the entrance at Sixth and Sansom, and was sent up to be interviewed by the lady in charge of personnel on the ninth floor. When she was on her way down, she heard Myron Kane had been killed. She got panicky and got off the elevator and came down the stairs. She saw a man dressed like Benjamin Franklin dodging into the phone booth, and she dodged into the women's washroom and waited till she heard him running up the stairs. She started on down, but she heard somebody coming up, so she dodged into the phone booth, and that's where she found the handkerchief."

"Does she say why it occurred to her that——"

It was as far as Colonel Primrose got. The sound of running feet came nearer on the other side of the door, out in the foyer, and the door burst open and a red-faced detective from the second division headquarters at 12th and Pine was there. And that's when we learned that Elsie Whitney Phelps' dead body had been found on the frozen bank of the Wissahickon, and that it had been there since shortly after noon, concealed behind a clump of laurel bushes. I think the strange part of it was that at that very moment Captain Malone had picked up the heavy bronze medallion with Franklin's head on one side and the Curtis Building on the other that in 1928 had commemorated the two-hundredth anniversary of *The Saturday Evening Post*, and that was now holding down some unfinished business on the side of Day Edgar's desk. He was turning it round and round in his hands, like a small heavy wheel. It was a mate to the one that had been used to put an end to Elsie's irritating but no doubt useful life.

Captain Malone sat there perfectly still for a moment, staring at the red-faced detective. He gathered his papers deliberately together, with the most remarkable composure, put them into his brief case and snapped it shut. He looked at Colonel Primrose.

"You may be on the right track, colonel. I don't know where Mr. Martin has been since he left Twelfth and Pine at ten thirty-five this morning. I'll get in touch with you later. Sorry I can't take you along now."

When Captain Malone had gone, Colonel Primrose sat there looking at the wall for a long time. He turned to me, his face troubled and very grave.

"I'm wondering if I could have saved her," he said. "I think not. She must have been a very stupid woman."

He went over to the window and stood looking down on Washington Square.

"They say it's greener than any other square because it was Potter's Field in Revolutionary times," he said. He was talking about the square, but I knew he wasn't thinking about it, and he didn't say anything else for quite a long time. Then he said, "It's strange the way a very bright man will believe anything a red-headed girl wants to tell him."

He turned around.

"I'm sorry about Elsie Phelps," he said quietly. "And about her husband. I hope Soapy Sam's alibi today is as watertight as the one he had yesterday."

I was still too shocked to say anything.

"We'd better go and see your friend Abigail," he said quietly. "I don't quite understand that old woman."

We went out through the swinging gate. It limped to a stop behind us. There was no one around until we got to the door going out to the elevators, and then a girl came quickly through the partition that closed off the row of editorial offices.

"Colonel Primrose," she said, "Mr. Martin would like to see you, if you have time."

Colonel Primrose nodded, and we followed her down the cork-floored corridor.

Pete Martin scrambled up from behind his desk. The ashtray was overflowing with quarter-smoked cigarettes, and his flushed, perspiring face looked strangely unrelated to the picture of himself in his age of innocence, in long dresses with a baby cap on his hairless head, that was propped up on the molding of the wall his desk was against. He didn't look at all like the star reporter and writer that he is.

"Why, look, colonel," he said. "I just stuck that outfit in Fred's file because the coast was clear down there." He grinned very sheepishly at us. "It was just a gag. I'm doing Warner Olivier's Keeping Posted this week while he's away, and I thought I'd dress up like Benjamin Franklin—as I did recently when I was working on an article on Hollywood make-up technique—and see what they'd do if the founder applied for a job during the manpower shortage. I was going to come up and get dressed, and go back down and tell Malone, but that's when I found out I'd bled all over the damned coat." He picked up a pair of paper scissors on his desk. "I did it with these when I was trying to trim the wig around my ears. I mopped it up with my handkerchief, but gee. . . . And the reason I came in through the ninth floor was that I didn't want to meet any of the gang. I was going to ask for an interview with an editor, to try to sell a treatise on lightning. I sure got all fouled up."

Colonel Primrose's face was grave still, but I could see his shoulders shaking slightly.

"I supposed you had," he said very urbanely. "I saw the piece you did on Hollywood make-up. You made a good Franklin." He smiled then. "There was a sentence at the end of another of your Hollywood articles that all of us should frame and remember. Something about a little ham in all of us? And they hang hams in Pennsylvania. Well, let's leave it as it is." He started out and turned. "You saw Kane when you crossed in front of the garden terrace, of course," he said. "What made you think he was dead?"

Pete Martin's large face flushed a little more. "He looked dead," he said reasonably. "I guess I ought to have yelled then, instead of going around the elevator shaft and coming in and pointing. But—well, I guess that's what happened to

142

me in Hollywood. But, colonel, I don't want to get Fred mixed up in this."

"Don't worry," Colonel Primrose said. At the door he turned back. "When you get the piece on roller skaters done, you'd better send a copy to Captain Malone. He's under a false impression."

15

"I don't quite know what to do," I said unhappily, as we came out through the plate-glass-and-bronze doors of the Curtis Building. "I hate to go back to Mrs. Whitney's, but I guess I ought to."

I might as well have been talking to the double row of stone columns. Colonel Primrose was so deep in his own concerns that mine were less than negligible. He was more profoundly disturbed than I'd ever seen him, and it gave me an increasingly uneasy feeling in the pit of my stomach. I'd got so used to having complete confidence in him that it frightened me a little, seeing him lose it in himself.

"I hope to God I'm not making a mistake," he said, with so much sincerity that my uneasiness quickened to alarm. He looked back at the Curtis Building.

"You don't really think it might be somebody there?"

"No, no, no," he said impatiently. "There wasn't the ghost of a motive, from the beginning. The mere fact that Kane was killed in the lobby——" He broke off abruptly. "I'm not worried about that. It's Toplady I'm thinking about." He looked toward Chestnut Street for the taxi that was supposed to come and pick us up. "If I'd known about Elsie Phelps, I'd have kept my mouth shut," he said grimly. "But Toplady would have come in for it sooner or later, or he'd have cracked up. And there's no time to work it out step by step, and they'd never get a conviction. Toplady would be dead and that would be the end of it."

I didn't understand a word he was saying, but the taxi came around the corner at that moment. If it hadn't, in another minute I'd have gone back and into the dispensary, and asked Doctor Repplier, the company physician, for a strait jacket.

He didn't have to tell me to be quiet this time. I was too disturbed to want to talk.

"Go on to Mrs. Whitney's and keep still," he said as we turned from Walnut Street into 17th. "Above all, don't say where you've been. Do you understand that?"

I nodded. He got out at the Warwick and disappeared under the green awning, and I went on around to the pink house on 19th Street.

The butler opened the door. "Madam wants to see you," he said. He wasn't smiling any more, and he didn't give the squirrel his walnut until I was halfway to the stairs, and then he did it rather surreptitiously and hastily closed the door.

I didn't think about the mirror until I'd got beyond it, so I didn't see Abigail until I was actually in her room.

"I'm so Glad you've come, Dear Child," she said.

She was alone and sitting up against the yellow cushions. She seemed very remote and detached, someway, with her battery of radios and telephones, books and flowers on the table beside her.

"It's rather horrible about Elsie," she said. "I'm more Distressed than I can say. I've implored her for years to mind her own business. I once gave her a *Blue-Back Speller* with the story about Tom, the Meddler, marked Very Clearly."

"When you and Sam said you had the document, you didn't, did you?" I asked.

She looked at me calmly. "I expected to have it and the manuscript this morning by Special Delivery. It was Fate. I've Always Believed in it. That's why I've shed very few tears in my life, Dear Child. What is to be, will be. It's very Silly to let yourself get Emotionally Involved. Nothing but Trouble comes of it."

She leaned her orange head back against the cushions and closed her eyes. She looked horribly old and saffron-colored, but still tensely alive.

"I don't wish anyone to—to be called to account for the death of either Myron Kane or Elsie Phelps," she said. Only her lips moved, and her voice was very quiet and clear. "There are various kinds of self-defense. One's reputation, and honor, and position in society, are more valuable than the mere breath animating a few pounds of water and clay."

Her eyes opened, and she looked directly at me.

"If someone has a knife at your throat and you kill him, it's justifiable homicide in self-defense. Both Myron Kane and Elsie held a knife, prepared to use it. Their departure was likewise justifiable homicide in self-defense."

I suppose it's a commentary on the kind of moral backbone I possess that when I was within her orbit, and under the

145

influence that she in her pink house and her brother in his brownstone one next door exerted, I felt there was a great deal in what she said. The only very real reservation I had was that I didn't want little Mr. Toplady also to bite the dust in justifiable homicide. I dare say she wouldn't regard his departure, if and when it was deemed necessary, as even an extreme length.

Her blue eyes were fixed on the mirror that reflected her tiny segment of the external world.

"Your friend, the Colonel, is going into my Brother's House," she said. "I regret having been Instrumental in bringing him here. I expect that was Fate, too, however. I didn't realize that, due to the Peculiar Intensity of Myron's animosity, matters were out of my hands. Myron was a terrible snob."

Her eyes were still on the mirror. Suddenly her fingers clenched and then began beating a soft tattoo on the green silk bedspread, slowly at first, faster, and then slowly again.

"I seldom smoke," she said, very quietly, "but I would like a cigarette now. You'll find one in the box on the table. . . . So Albert Toplady is finally coming to see me."

I was getting her a gold-tipped Turkish cigarette out of the silver box when she said that. I turned quickly. She was watching the mirror, intent as a cat, her fingers drumming slowly and irregularly as a cat's tail twitching.

I remembered everything Colonel Primrose had told me, but I couldn't help it. "Do you know Mr. Toplady?" I inquired as casually as I could.

"At one time I had considerable dealings with him."

I don't know and never shall know why I had to go on. "And you knew he is Myron Kane's father."

She stared at me, her eyes aghast and unbelieving, her face drained suddenly of every vestige of color, her mouth open.

"I—I thought you knew!" I stammered. "I thought the letter——"

She straightened up slowly. "There was nothing in the letter," she said sharply. "It was just fan mail—just what you said it was. The reason we had to—had to see it was we thought Toplady might be trying to sell Myron Kane information, knowing he was doing an article on my brother."

She leaned back again against her cushions, her eyes closed, and lay there so still that I thought she might have fainted. Then she opened her eyes. She put her hand out.

"That makes it very different," she whispered. "Get my

146

Brother. Tell him to come quickly. I have to see him." She motioned toward the phone. "Tell him to come alone. Tell him I'm dying. He'll be Delighted."

I started toward the phone, but I didn't call Judge Whitney. I hadn't heard the door being answered or seen anyone in the mirror outside, but there in the door was Monk Whitney. He was in uniform and he had an overcoat and bag. He put the bag down and threw the coat on top of it and came over to the foot of the swan bed. He moved slowly, like a man struggling in some inner hell, his eyes haggard.

"I've come to say good-by, Aunt Abby," he said. "I'm leaving."

Her face was some kind of a mask so far outside my experience that I couldn't attempt to interpret it.

She was silent for a long time, just looking at him.

"I think you should stay," she said then, calmly.

He shook his head. "He'll have Travis and Laurel," he said. "If he should need me, I'll come. I'd rather—I mean——"

"I know what you mean." Her eyes were fixed steadily on him. "Where are they now?"

"Over at the house, all of them. They just brought Sam over. I never thought I'd see a guy cry like that. He was out looking for her every place. His secretaries were calling up everybody she knew. How much—I mean, did he know what——" He found the going too hard, and stopped.

"Do you mean," his aunt said very quietly, "did he know what was in the document Elsie intercepted? No. Unless she got in touch with him and told him. Which I doubt."

"Are you sure?"

"I'm too old to be sure of anything, Dear Boy," she said. "He was probably merely using his head. It was I who asked him to phone this Dear Child's house and have her maid forward Myron's mail. I presume he put two and two together, and knew Elsie had assumed a danger as great as Myron's."

Abigail Whitney was watching him intently, her eyes suddenly brilliant pin points of blue fire, and crafty blue fire. She relaxed suddenly, her frail body sunk back against the cushions, her face as bland as a desiccated Buddha's.

"Where is that little creature Albert Toplady?" she asked calmly.

"At the house," Monk said. "Well, I guess I'll shove. Good-by, Aunt Abby. . . . Good-by, Grace. Stand by, will you?"

The appeal in his eyes was eloquent far above and beyond

147

anything he could have said. It was bewildering to me, because it didn't seem credible that he could believe his father, Judge Nathaniel Whitney, could——

"They're coming." Abigail's voice was as sharp as a lancet. "Go quickly."

The blue eyes were intent and crafty again. I don't know how or why, but I knew, with a flash of intuitive certainty as clear as lightning against a summer sky, that she was planning, someway, to sell him out.

"Don't go, Monk!" The words came out of my mouth before I was aware of even thinking of saying them.

He stopped short halfway across the room and turned back. He couldn't have helped catch the malignant glance Abigail Whitney shot me before she settled back in her yellow cushions.

"It is too late to do anything, Dear Boy," she said calmly. "They're here, I'm afraid."

I looked quickly in her outside mirror. The street was empty. I looked at her. Her eyes were fixed on the other mirror—the one by the door on the wall. In it I could see the shell recess in the hall outside. The whole shell was moving, swinging open, and as it moved I saw a narrow corridor that was full of men. Judge Whitney's white head towered above them all. Then they were in the hall, crowding the mirror. In front were Colonel Primrose, Albert Toplady and Judge Whitney. Mr. Toplady was staring around him like a frail awed soul newly admitted through the paradisial gates.

Abigail Whitney's fingers drummed silently on the green silk cover and were motionless. Judge Whitney's deep, grave voice came in from the hall. "He said he was coming over here."

Monk stood silently by the window, facing them.

"He is probably with Mrs. Whitney," Colonel Primrose said.

He looked at the door. It seemed to me that his eyes and old Abigail's met in the mirror and held an instant before he turned away. "Perhaps you'd better see, Malone."

Captain Malone's head showed over Mr. Toplady's. He came to the door.

"I'm here, if you want me," Monk said evenly.

I heard Colonel Primrose's voice again from the hall. "All right, Mr. Toplady. Will you wait back there in the library until we're ready for you?"

Captain Malone turned in the doorway. "You ought to have somebody wait with him," he said dryly.

148

"If you think so." I thought Colonel Primrose's voice sounded a little annoyed. "Will someone——"

"I will, if you'd like me to."

I hadn't seen Laurel Frazier anywhere, and her voice came as a surprise to me. And to Monk Whitney. He moved abruptly and was motionless again, his face going tight and shuttered.

"Travis can stay, colonel," Judge Whitney said.

"I'll be glad to, sir," Travis Elliot said. "If you'll see they aren't too rough on Aunt Abby."

I glanced at Aunt Abby. A faint smile moved at one corner of her mouth. She settled back for all the world like a cat curling down on a cushion in front of a fire.

"Very well," Colonel Primrose said. "You can close the door, Elliot. I want a few words first with Mrs. Whitney."

In some way that seemed incredible to me, Abigail had managed to smooth out her face and soften her eyes and look the ultimate in a fragile invalidism that the first rude breath would end forever. If ever I saw a sepulcher so freshly and perfectly whited in my very presence, I can't recall it.

Monk glanced at her and at me, the lift of his eyebrows hardly perceptible. Then they were coming in.

It's hard to get what happened then so that it makes factual sense, it all happened so quickly. One minute Abigail was lying back against her yellow cushions, a calm and controlled, if faded, shadow. The next her face was saffron again, the lines in it carved deeply and terribly, all her pretense about not becoming Emotionally Involved lying in wretched tatters about her, a stricken old spider with her web torn apart, useless to protect the only thing she loved. Judge Whitney came in, grave and dignified, and as secure as if he were wearing his judicial robes, and in an instant he was gray and haggard, his hand reaching blindly out for a chair or anything to keep him from utter physical collapse. It happened to all of them except to Laurel Frazier, and that was because she'd come in, her bright copper hair like a flame that had burned all the life from her body, moving erect and taut, her lips parted a little, her eyes dulled and gray, waiting for some blow to fall. And Monk Whitney stood motionless by the window.

Colonel Primrose came in, passing a foot in front of me without so much as a glance in my direction, and went directly to Abigail Whitney's stately and lovely swan bed. She looked up at him with so much concentrated charm in those vivid cornflower eyes that I wondered for an instant if

149

she'd got herself mixed up with Madame de Sévigné, or whoever it was who still had lovers at ninety. She held out her hand.

"I am honored, colonel," she murmured. "I've seldom——"

His hands held hers for a bare instant and moved down to her bedside table. He picked up an ivory-painted radio. Abigail's hand poised in the air was rigid, her body erect. The limpid eyes, cornflower blue, were black as a cobra's.

"The blue dial, colonel," she said. Her voice was clear and sharp.

Their eyes met for an instant.

"I think not, Mrs. Whitney," he said politely.

His fingers went to the red dial, and turned it quickly.

That was when she changed, sooner than the rest, because she knew. And I knew, too, then. I knew how she'd heard everything Myron Kane had said to me, how she knew the carbon copy of the manuscript and the document that Laurel had given him by mistake out of Judge Whitney's files were at my house in Georgetown, and how she knew I'd called her a scheming, worldly old woman. The red dial tuned her in to every conversation that went on in the house. The blue dial went the other way. It was the one I'd seen her fiddle with when she told me she didn't want a useful life destroyed. It had let Laurel Frazier hear every word she'd said then, and it had been on the night I'd heard Judge Whitney's voice in my room for a brief moment before she'd switched it off. That was why no servant ever had to appear upstairs for an order. And I knew now why she wanted the blue dial turned on, and why, when Colonel Primrose turned the red dial, she collapsed back against the cushions, old and saffron and destroyed, even before we heard Travis Elliot's voice in the library.

He was speaking very quietly, but his voice came with a horrible and ghastly clarity. ". . . a break I really didn't expect, Mr. Toplady. I'm playing in luck these days, it seems."

The calm, confident voice, tinged with amused arrogance, came out of the ivory box so perfectly that I found myself not hearing it, but seeing Travis Elliot standing there, poised and entirely controlled, as he'd been standing when I came into this room the first time.

"Where are they, Mr. Toplady? You brought them, didn't you?" His voice sharpened for an instant. "Good. And let's be quick about it. You're sure they're all here?"

There was a long silence—in both rooms.

The voice came out of the ivory box again. "It's too bad I can't see for myself, Mr. Toplady. But I don't think you'd have the guts to pull a fast one—not when you're in for the five thousand Abigail gave you to protect my father's good name. It's funny I never thought about this. Not till today, when the good colonel spilled it at the table. So he saw the records of the Elliot steal, did he? And you didn't talk, did you, Mr. Toplady?"

When the little man's voice came out of the ivory box for the first time, the contrast to Travis Elliot's cool, articulate confidence was so frightening that I felt a cold dread around my heart. And yet, shaking and hardly audible as it was, it had a kind of dignity and courage—I suppose of a man who knew he was utterly lost.

"He saw them. I—I couldn't help it. They were on the same film he was looking at."

"He couldn't tell anything," the coolly amused voice said.

"Yes, he could. If he knew about signatures."

Travis' voice sharpened again instantly. "What do you mean, Mr. Toplady?"

"I mean because of your father's heart. You can see it—it shows in a person's signature. Bookkeepers can tell lots of times before a man suspects it himself or the doctor does. That's how I knew it wasn't your father signing the checks against Miss Frazier's money. The signature looked the same but for that. I found out you'd opened a Number Two Account in his name. You presented a letter he was supposed to have signed. But it wasn't his signature. It was yours—you had no heart condition. I didn't know what to do. It would have raised such a scandal at the company. So—so I went to him and told him about it myself."

There was a silence again.

"Well, it won't matter now, will it, Mr. Toplady?" the cool voice said. "Here they go, and they burn nicely, don't they? Much better than paper, Mr. Toplady."

Then there was a sudden gasp, and a small cry like the cry of some terrified little animal.

"I don't want to do this, Mr. Toplady," Travis Elliot said, "but there's nothing else I can do. The walls are thick and the doors closed. Primrose and Malone are busy in there. Primrose has been getting his dope from the charming Mrs. Latham, and she and Monk and my future wife all think it was the judge. Because—thanks to Aunt Abby—they all think he murdered my father. And Malone doesn't know I was an office boy at the *Post* one summer, the year they got out the medals for the two-hundredth anniversary. And part of my job was taking manuscripts up to the composing room when the pneumatic tubes got clogged. It's too bad I can't tie you up with the *Post*, too, Mr. Toplady. I'm afraid you'll just have to be a suicide. The powder marks will show the gun was close to your forehead, and your prints will be on it. Nothing against you personally, Mr. Toplady, but I didn't have anything against Kane. Or Elsie, except she was so damned officious. Even calling me up to tell me——"

His voice changed suddenly into a snarl that was nothing human. I stood there perfectly paralyzed and frozen-hearted, and I remember turning with a kind of despair to Colonel Primrose.

"Oh, can't you do something?" I cried.

Then Sam Phelps was running toward the door, his face convulsed, and Captain Malone caught him and held him, wrestling with him, just as the gunshot cracked and we heard a crash and a sound like brass fire irons clanging on a brick hearth. Monk started toward the door and stopped as Colonel Primrose shook his head.

And Colonel Primrose stood there, imperturbable and undisturbed, and reached down and turned on the blue dial.

"Well, Buck?" he said.

And I could have wept as I heard that composed granite voice coming out of the little ivory box. "Everything as ordered, sir," Sergeant Buck said. Then there was a tinge of something like apology in his sinister tones, as if it wasn't quite as ordered, after all.

"I had to knock the son of a—the fellow out. Little man's okay. Shot missed him, winged the looking glass. Captain Malone——"

Colonel Primrose switched off the red dial. The room was suddenly silent, except for Captain Malone's swift strides and the metallic clink of the handcuffs against the doorknob and the door banging shut after him.

Laurel Frazier hadn't moved since she came into the room. The color was coming slowly back into her cheeks and the blue was deepening the gray of her eyes again. Monk was looking at her, his face full of a compassion and tenderness that was very moving. He went over to her slowly and put both hands on her shoulders. "I'm sorry, Coppertop," he said gently.

She looked up at him silently for a moment. Then she said, "I was just—just afraid it—maybe it was you. Oh, Monk, don't be horrid to me any more!"

She was in his arms then, her burnished head by those starred ribbons, and he was holding her close to him. And I turned away just in time to see Colonel Primrose going out into the hall. I followed him, and saw the two of them coming from the library. I've forgotten who it was—Moses, I imagine—who brought water out of the solid rock. Miracles, I suppose, like history, repeat themselves, because Sergeant Buck was actually mopping his granite forehead with his sleeve. His other huge arm was round Mr. Albert Toplady's frail shoulders.

I turned back. Monk held Laurel's arms in his hands and bent down and kissed her. He went over then to his father and put his hand on his shoulder. Judge Whitney raised his head. They didn't say anything. After a moment, Judge Whitney got slowly to his feet and looked across the room at his sister.

"Well, Abigail?" he said quietly.

Colonel Primrose came back into the room. Outside in the hall I heard the tread of heavy feet, and I turned away quickly. Colonel Primrose closed the door, looking from Judge Whitney to his sister.

Abigail Whitney straightened up against her yellow cushions, but her blue eyes were old and tired. The alchemy was there no longer.

"You did kill Douglas Elliot," she said, her voice slow and painful. "When you came to me to borrow the money to make up the loss—— Oh, if you had only told me it was for him, not for you! You said you needed it; you didn't say Douglas needed it. If you'd said it was for Douglas I would have given it willingly, and then he would never have had to take his own life. He'd never have had to make the sacrifice he did to shield his son. It was morally you that killed him, Nathaniel, even though the gun was in his own hand."

"You wouldn't have lent this money to your own brother?" Colonel Primrose asked quietly.

The blue fire blazed up in her eyes. "Never! If it had not been for my brother I would have married Douglas Elliot, and Travis would have been my child. Money was all I ever got out of marriage. I would have died before I let my brother profit by a single dollar of it."

"I would have told you," Judge Whitney said slowly, "if I had known he was going to take his life. I would have broken my word to him. He made me swear solemnly that I would not tell you it was for him. I didn't realize that it was his last resort and there was no other way out. I—it may be that I was wrong in not letting him marry you. Money seemed to be all you ever wanted, and you would have ruined him in making him get it for you. . . . What was this document that Myron Kane got?"

A touch of her old manner came back to her. She sat up straighter.

"It's most Unfortunate," she said. "It was a letter Douglas wrote to you. He posted it before he . . . killed himself. It came the morning after. I—I did what Elsie did. I signed for it and I read it. I should have burned it, but it was his last word, and I—I never dared." She closed her eyes for a moment, the tears rolling down her wasted yellow cheeks. "It said the envelope enclosed in it was being entrusted to you. You were to look after Travis. If he was ever in trouble of his own making, you were to open it. I opened it then—like Elsie. It said he was taking the blame for the loss of Laurel's money. He wanted to save his son from disgrace and give him another chance. It was the only way he knew. He was doing it because he loved him, and it may have been his fault for giving him responsibility beyond his years. He said he had told Travis he was leaving a statement of the truth with someone, not telling him who, so Travis would never go wrong again. He said the man Toplady would know. All he was trying to do was protect Travis against temptation again."

"And you put the letter in my files?" Judge Whitney asked.

"I put it there. I was afraid not to. I thought you would take it out to Whitemarsh and nobody would ever disturb it until we were dead. I've left all my property to Travis, and I left word for him where to find the letter when I'm gone. He's all I've . . . ever had." Abigail Whitney's eyes closed again.

"You knew he was going to kill Myron Kane?" Colonel Primrose asked deliberately.

She opened her eyes quickly. "No, no. I was trying to save him, just as I tried to save Elsie. I didn't want their blood on his hands. But afterward there was nothing I could do. And now, please go, all of you. I am Very Tired."

16

I didn't see Abigail Whitney again, and I didn't want to. I did see Monk and Laurel, because they were married at Judge Whitney's, and she's like a lot of other people now, living in a tourist cabin near a marine station, waiting for Monk to go across again before she goes back to her job with his father. It wasn't till after the marriage that she told Colonel Primrose she really had tried to get a job at the *Post*, thinking she might be able to get hold of the manuscript. It was all she could think of to do to try to save Judge Whitney. And it was Sergeant Buck who'd found her in the telephone booth and got her out.

I didn't see the people at *The Saturday Evening Post* again, either, but it seems Colonel Primrose did. We were going down to Washington on the train.

"I don't like to admit it, of course," I said, "but I owe you a real apology. I didn't for a minute realize you were deliberately bringing up the Douglas steal at Judge Whitney's luncheon."

Colonel Primrose smiled a little.

"And how did you know about Abigail's communication system?"

"I spotted the vent in the molding in that downstairs reception room the day I called for you," he said placidly. "Buck followed up via the butler and the maid and the electrician who installed it. It was very simple."

"Maybe," I said dubiously. "There's another thing that may be simple to you, but not to me. That's how Travis ever got Myron murdered and stuck in the pool. He said he'd worked at the *Post*, but——"

Colonel Primrose had a wry half-smile on one side of his face. "That's the trouble of being off the home field," he said. "In Washington I'd have known everything Captain Lamb

155

knew. Malone wasn't playing it that way. I'd never got to first base if I hadn't met up with Mr. Toplady. Malone, on the other hand, had Travis pretty well traced down, except he didn't know it was Travis. He was still trying to pin it on somebody at the *Post*—or on Monk, at the end. Travis was still cocky enough when they got him to headquarters to correct Malone on a few minor points, but, in the main, Malone was right.

"What happened was that Travis had an appointment to meet Myron in the lobby at two-thirty. Myron was to get the script and give it to him. But Myron, as you remember, hadn't got it—Bob Fuoss told him to wait for the proof. But Travis knew the ropes. It was he who called up Composition in the morning, said he was W. Thornton Martin, and was told the manuscript had gone to the monotype keyboard. He knew the place would be deserted at noon, when they all went to lunch. He walked in the lobby and across to the second-register elevator, went up to the fifth floor and through to the manufacturing side, took off his coat, rolled up his sleeves and went up on the elevator to the ninth floor. He says he didn't have any idea of doing anything but get the script, and settle with Myron later, but when he went through the foundry, he saw the cutting-down knife lying where Albert Hesington had left it when he went to lunch.

"He says he didn't plan at that point to stay in the building, but people started to come back. So he calmly went into that phone booth—you remember, where we went along with Mr. Trayser to get to the runway from Manufacturing to the lunchroom on the editorial side on the ninth floor. Every time anybody came along, he was busy apparently making phone calls. He waited until time to meet Myron, picked up his coat and hat, that he'd left on the fifth floor, and went on down. He says that even then he didn't plan to kill Myron there. But Myron was standing up on the terrace, looking at the mosaic, and they were hidden from the desk by the pillars and the shrubbery. The lobby was empty and the elevators had both just gone up, and he recognized it was a natural. Myron turned to face him and he just let him have it. The knife was pointed and razor-sharp. He left it in and lowered Myron's body into the pool, face down, and walked off."

Colonel Primrose shook his head.

"He didn't realize, until he was outside, how neatly he'd laid it all on the *Post*'s doorstep. It seemed to amuse him considerably. And he was civil enough to say he hoped Pete

156

Martin wouldn't hold it against him; he'd used his name because he'd just read one of his articles. The fact that his initials and Monk's were the same was pure coincidence."

Colonel Primrose was silent for a moment. "And by the way," he went on, "I had lunch with Marion Turner and Hibbs and Erd Brandt. They tell me a good many of their readers think this has gone far enough. They think you ought to marry me and get it over with."

I picked up a copy of the *Post* the man next to me had left in his seat when he went to dinner, and opened it. Sergeant Buck, fortunately, was a dozen seats away at the end of the car.

Colonel Primrose looked at me and smiled. "Well?" he said.

www.ingramcontent.com/pod-product-compliance
Lightning Source LLC
Chambersburg PA
CBHW022132170626
46808CB00002B/966